D1509111

THE IRON WEB

Also by Ken Crowder

The Colter Conspiracy

The Iron Web

Ken Crowder

Walker and Company ✺ New York

First published in the United States of America
in 1985 by the Walker Publishing Company, Inc.

Published simultaneously in Canada by John Wiley & Sons
Canada, Limited, Rexdale, Ontario.

Book Design by Teresa M. Carboni

Library of Congress Cataloging in Publication Data

Crowder, Ken, 1944–
    The iron web.

    1. World War, 1939–1945--Fiction. I. Title.
PS3553.R588I7 1985   813'.54   85-2294
ISBN 0-8027-0846-3

Printed in the United States of America

10 9 8 7 6 5 4 3 2 1

THE IRON WEB

1

ABWEHR CAPTAIN AUGUST Diels leaned back in his swivel chair, hands behind his neck. The all-clear warning had sounded a little while ago and they had emerged from the cellar of their Berlin headquarters building to resume the day's work. August Diels was superintendent of the Abwehr's Unit D, military intelligence relating to Baltic activity. He wore his uniform uneasily. A small, hunched-shouldered man with thick glasses, Diels had been an accountant before the war and was still an accountant at heart.

The Abwehr, the intelligence arm of the *Oberkommando der Wehrmacht*, had changed greatly since Diels had rather reluctantly, under his father's insistence, become a part of it.

Formerly, Diels had supervised a network of agents along the Baltic coast and at sea, receiving intelligence reports—sightings, radio intercept, reports obtained through infiltrated anti-Nazi groups. These reports, sifted to eliminate the obvious chaff and disinformation planted by the Allies, were passed through Diels on to the OKW, the high command of the armed forces.

These days there was little enough coming in. The Allies had control of the Baltic, and most of Diels's agents in the field had been captured or had disappeared—many, Diels secretly believed, going over voluntarily. The thick intelligence-briefing folders Diels had formerly turned in regularly had diminished to an occasional one- or two-sheet bulletin. Each of which carried worse news than the one before.

"Can you watch my desk for me, August?" asked the red-faced man across from Diels in the cluttered office. Diels nodded, letting no expression show on his face. In the street below, a fire truck clanged past toward the north, where the Allied bombing—British by night, American by day—had been the most intense.

Albert Bruckman, the red-faced man, rose from his desk, popping a clove into his mouth to neutralize his halitosis, a product of rotting teeth; who had seen a dentist in Berlin in late 1943?

Then he was off, with a sly wink at Diels. He usually met Helga, the heavy, sweatered blonde from communications, at this hour on Wednesdays. They went to the furnace room and rubbed themselves violently against each other, perhaps trying to banish the war in that way.

The door closed and August Diels looked around slowly. Then, casually, he walked to Bruckman's desk, lifting the telephone receiver and tucking it between shoulder and chin so that if someone came in he could say that Bruckman's phone had rung.

It was lunchtime. Bruckman always met the woman at lunchtime. No one else was in the office. August Diels sorted through Bruckman's work, careful not to rearrange the folders on his desk. He found the two he sought beneath a report on the Leningrad ghetto. Carefully Diels slid them out, noting the carefully printed labels: *Dachau* and *Auschwitz*. Apparently, there was nothing new at Buchenwald, Mauthausen, Sachsenhausen, or Treblinka this week.

Diels glanced inside, seeing only numbers and names. The Dachau report for this week didn't even have names, only the cold black numbers: *1,664 Jews and Communists relocated, bringing our total to 7,043 for this month and 24,000 persons for this reporting period.* The Dachau folder also contained a report from Dr. Sigmund Rascher. This information, he claimed, was vital to the survival of German airmen who might be downed in the sea under extreme climatic conditions. Diels scanned a part of it.

The test persons were chilled in the familiar way—dressed or undressed—in cold water at various temperatures. Removal from the water took place at a rectal temperature of 86 degrees.

2

In eight cases the test persons were placed between two naked women on a wide bed. The rise in body temperature then proceeded at approximately the same speed as with test persons warmed by being swathed in blankets. An exception was formed by four test persons who practiced sexual intercourse between 86 and 89.5 degrees. In three persons after coitus, a very swift temperature rise ensued, comparable to that achieved by means of a hot water bath.

Each prisoner was placed naked on a stretcher outside the barracks in the evening. He was covered with a sheet, and every hour a bucket of cold water was poured over him. The test person lay out like this into the morning. Their temperatures were taken.

Initially, these tests were made without anesthetic, but the test persons made such a racket that it was impossible to continue these tests without—

The door opened and Diels leaned back, absently fingering the reports.

"Yes, Herr Major," he said heartily, speaking into the telephone as he leaned back. "One minute, please, someone is in the room."

The humorless, tight-lipped female secretary who had come into the room turned on a heel and went out immediately, slamming the door behind her.

Diels half-smiled and got back to the folders. He wanted to read no more. He looked at the sticker pasted to the upper righthand corner of each folder, saw that Bruckman had checked only the Dachau folder with his distinctive violet ink. This folder, then, was the only one which had been completely read, and was ready for filing.

Diels lifted his eyes to the door, opened the folder again, and quickly, deftly, removed the second copy from the Dachau folder. That done, he returned to his desk and pored over his sketchy Baltic reports until Bruckman, looking satisfied and reeking of cheap perfume, returned.

"Watch my desk, please," Diels said. "I haven't eaten."

He went out then into the broad, wood-paneled corridor

where each door was guarded by a soldier with an automatic weapon. His boot heels rang against the oak parquet as he strode toward the stairs, the Dachau report in his pocket, a sheaf of Baltic reports enclosed in a folder he carried in his right hand.

He entered the lavatory and went into a booth, closing the door. There the Dachau report was added to the papers in his folder. He heard two men enter and recognized the voice of one of them: SD Major Birger Buehler. Diels frowned, flushed the commode, and went out. Buehler's stony face turned toward him.

"Ah, Diels, how are things in the Baltic?"

"For you or for the Führer?"

Buehler laughed, but there was a distant light in his eyes that Diels didn't care for. He washed up quickly and went out. Down the hall he found the courier sacks ready to be loaded, each tagged for its destination. In the corner sat a pile of similar bags for future use. If there was any future use. There were few stations of the Abwehr now operating outside the country, and there would be fewer tomorrow.

"Nothing for France—anywhere in France," Heinz Mueller said. "Oh, it's you, Diels. You're just in time. The truck is ready to roll out to Rangsdorf. How's your father?"

"We don't write outside of this," Diels said, hurriedly filling out a destination card. That handed to Mueller, the folder he carried was sealed in an oilskin packet and placed in a nearby olive-drab sack, which Mueller fastened by running a padlock with an overlong hasp through the brass grommets fitted to the top.

"One more, Karl!" Mueller shouted, and with relief Diels saw the perspiring corporal, a man of some years, heft the sack and carry it out to the waiting truck.

"I'll soon be out of a job," Mueller said, straightening up, holding his back. "Do you know how many courier planes are left? Six!" He held up six stubby fingers. "Out of one hundred and nine. We have six. Four are those toy airplanes, those . . ."

"Fieseler-Storches," Diels provided.

"Yes, well it's a wonder they fly your stuff to your father."

"There's a regular supply plane out of Libya."

"Is there? There won't be any of our planes flying out of Libya for long, I'll wager," Mueller said, lifting his eyes to the door. One didn't like to be overheard expressing sentiments like that.

"No," Diels said, "not for much longer at all. Good day, Mueller." The older man lifted a hand, and Diels went out, feeling relieved of his burden. The dispatch was on its way to Rangsdorf Airfield. From there it would be taken to Brindisi, Italy, then across the Mediterranean by a night fighter. If the field at Baida was still intact and still held by German forces, if they were still flying supplies south, then August Diels's father would receive his dispatch in four to five days. But there would be no more. Diels decided that just then. It was far too risky. All lines of communication and travel were subject to disruption. It was much too chancy. If one of those bags came back to Abwehr headquarters and was inspected, it would be the end. Buehler would have him over in the basement at SD headquarters in five minutes. Bastards. He saw Buehler and one of his henchmen still standing in the hallway as he walked back toward his office. Yet they would learn nothing. The last dispatch was gone and there would be no more. August Diels was able to whistle and greet Buehler cheerfully again as he passed the SD men.

Buehler, hands behind his waist, watched. "He's up to something."

"Diels, Herr Major?"

"Yes. I don't know what, but he's up to something. I'd like to talk to him."

"The Constitution—"

"Yes," Buehler snapped. "We have no control over the Abwehr. Not now. But perhaps there will come a time, eh, Herr Lieutenant?"

"If Field Marshal Goering has his way, yes."

"I live for that day. If these bastards in the Abwehr aren't traitors, they're the next thing to it. They're just plain incompetent. Criminally so. I ask you, if we had decent intelligence, would we be losing this damned war?"

The lieutenant, who knew Buehler had never been within a hundred miles of the front, said he supposed not. He supposed Himmler's SD should handle intelligence. Who could trust the army OKW these days? It was then that the sirens began to wail again and they headed for the basement, hearing the first distant rumbling of an approaching American bomber wing.

Latitude 62° 15' N, Longitude 9° 57' W, off the Faroe Islands in the south Norwegian Sea. High seas and rolling gray skies with the wind from the northwest at Force 6-8.

The convoy was a lumbering, laboring thing, stretched out endlessly. The U-214 maintained its parallel course a thousand meters off the port flank of the Russia-bound convoy. The periscope was blocked by heavy seas washing over it, and at this depth even the Unterseeboot felt the tug and push of the heavy seas. The boat corkscrewed and pitched as she stalked the convoy, her commander, Oberleutnant Peter Karl Neff, Count von Roenne, at the scope, his arms limp as he draped himself over it, his eyes coldly intent.

He could make out three oil tankers, two large freighters, two American destroyers, and a Royal Navy MTB, which was being tossed about rather badly by mountainous seas. Great pyramid-shaped, white-topped waves constantly crossed his line of vision.

"They've seen us, sir," Fritzche said suddenly, not with excitement, but matter-of-factly. This business no longer held any excitement. Von Roenne had lost two submarines already; scores of men had been killed. Fritzche, the second watch officer, was merely reflecting his superior's attitude—that they would die at sea. Sooner or later they would all die.

"Eight hundred meters, sir," von Roenne was advised. The

oberleutnant still peered into his periscope as if he were merely passing time.

"Forward tubes ready," he said tonelessly. "Activate TDC." This was a complicated electrical device linking the gyro compass, attack periscope, and torpedo circuit.

"Activated," the leading seaman called back.

Von Roenne still hung over the periscope's handles, recalling 'forty and 'forty-one, when this had all been so easy. So simple it had nearly seemed unlawful. Since then the Allied radar had been perfected; now they knew where the U-boats were. In 1942 German U-boats had sunk six and a quarter million tons of Allied shipping, but beginning in 'forty-three—thanks to improved techniques utilizing long-range aircraft, carriers, and shipboard radar—the death knell from U-boat warfare had been sounded. In February, March, and April of 1943, fifty U-boats had been sunk. In May alone, thirty-seven. In September, U-boats had killed sixty-seven Allied vessels—at the cost of sixty-four submarines.

In a rage, the Führer had removed Grand Admiral Raeder from his post as commander-in-chief of the Kriegsmarine, replacing him with Admiral Karl Doenitz, who could do no more to stem the tide than Raeder. Materiel still flowed toward Russia. The factories, harassed constantly by Allied bombers, couldn't hope to keep pace with Germany's terrific losses in the Atlantic.

"Five hundred meters."

Von Roenne settled the aiming cross of the periscope on the gray bulk of the first destroyer's bow. "Line of sight," he called. "Prepare port bow torpedoes for firing."

"Three hundred meters."

"Fire one and two."

The submarine lurched as the two torpedoes were expelled and raced silently toward the homing destroyer. Von Roenne, pinned to his periscope, watched as the American ship bore down on them. He could see men on the bridge, wearing orange lifejackets and steel helmets. Then he saw the gushing orange flames, saw the destroyer seem to heel over almost instantly.

"Down scope, run at fifty meters," von Roenne said, turning. "Course oh-nine-oh."

"We're pursuing?" Fritzche asked, his concern showing only slightly. There was a tenseness around his mouth, a flicker of cold light in his brown eyes.

"Of course," said von Roenne. Amazingly, he yawned. Fritzche spent a moment looking at his superior officer. From a family of wealth and influence, he had taken a degree in philosophy at Heidelberg, graduating before he was twenty. He had driven racing cars on the European Grand Prix circuit, was a good enough rifle shot to have tried out for the Olympics.

Von Roenne was now thirty years of age. He had been a submarine commander for four years, one of the few to survive so long in what had become a suicidal business. He was tall, narrow, fair, with pale blue eyes and a haughty, or perhaps bored, expression. A terrible scar crossed his forehead from side to side—the result of a depth-charge attack on his second command. During the loss of his third ship, which had foundered on the shallows off Jutland, and from which von Roenne and thirty of his men had swum while searching fire probed the night, the captain had lost three fingers of his right hand, torn free as he tried to yank a seaman up through a twisted, jagged hatch.

He limped severely, but Fritzche was not certain how that had been caused—he thought it was from a racing-car accident.

Von Roenne now wore a white undershirt and blue coveralls like the rest of the crew. He had on a battered, white-topped naval cap, and around his neck was the knight's cross with oak leaves, a rare distinction given by the Führer's own hand for conspicuous gallantry.

"Here she comes over," said Langer, the chief helmsman. He wore headphones and a throat microphone. Listening now, they could hear the destroyer overhead. All eyes lifted.

"Dive, sir?"

8

"No," von Roenne answered, "pass under her. Stay on course."

There was no argument. A distant muffled explosion sounded, and then one not so distant made their ears ring and the submarine roll.

"Directly overhead, sir."

Fritzche felt the sweat running off his neck and back. They were under the destroyer, and von Roenne was accepting a cup of coffee from the huge, tattooed chief engineer, Rudi Johst. Johst had been with von Roenne from the beginning, and just now his main concern seemed to be that the count should not spill his coffee due to the annoying vibrations from the depth charge.

Von Roenne took a sip and handed the cup back. "Periscope depth."

Fritzche felt his stomach tighten. Von Roenne was going up. He was going to attack the convoy with the destroyer on top of them. No one argued. No one spoke. Perhaps they had come to believe von Roenne was immortal; or perhaps they had all simply resigned themselves to death beside him.

Von Roenne hunched down over the periscope again, and Fritzche heard an indefinite hiss escape the captain's teeth. The periscope broke water, and there was the convoy. Von Roenne marked the last tanker in line, and the starboard torpedoes slithered away in angry flight.

"Dive. Thirty degrees," von Roenne said immediately. They could hear the destroyer coming about, in hot pursuit. Then there was a huge, distant explosion, audible above the surface wind, through the water and the steel hull of the U-214.

"The tanker!" Fritzche said jubilantly. Still the destroyer was closing.

"Stern torpedo tube ready!" von Roenne commanded, even his usually imperturbable voice at last excited.

"Ready."

"Fire!"

Again the U-boat rocked as the stern torpedo jetted away. "Count ten," the captain said to Fritzche, rubbing his head.

9

"If you don't hear something by then, I'm afraid we've had it."

Fritzche had only gotten to nine when they heard the second explosion. They had tagged the destroyer with the stern torpedo. A rousing cheer went up, echoing through the submarine. Von Roenne ordered the U-214 leveled, and stretched out his hand for the coffee cup.

"She's not heeding, sir," the chief helmsman called. "Bowplanes damaged, I think."

And then Fritzche thought he saw what he had never seen before in those so-pale blue eyes von Roenne turned on them all—anger. He had a half dozen torpedoes left, ready to aim at an enemy convoy, fat lazy freighters, their bellies bloated with fuel oil. And a disabled boat.

He handed his cup to Johst and took the controls himself, yanking mightily on the obviously jammed diving planes. Then, with a smothered curse, von Roenne turned away.

"I'll be in my quarters, Fritzche. Away ballast, head her in for Wilhelmshaven."

"Aye, sir."

Then he was gone, limping away, his face suffused with blood. And to the north the convoy chugged away, carrying fuel from Canada and the United States for Archangel.

"What is it, Rudi?" Fritzche asked the chief engineer. "Is it that they've gotten away, is he angry because he could have scored three more kills?"

"You have to ask me, sir?" Rudi Johst asked, grinning. "It is partly as you say, but mostly I think it is that they have wounded his ship. They wound the count when they damage his ship. Down here"—a massive arm moved in a gesture— "he can control his destiny—our destinies. The world is very small here, well ordered if deadly. Up above—what is that but mad chaos? Only a madman can think he controls what goes on up there. It is not war so much as an eruption of horrors."

"But he has lost another boat. So now what is there for the rest of us to do, Rudi?"

"I think," the big man said cheerfully, "a small vacation, many women, and much beer." Then he saluted in a way that was both respectful and friendly, and turned to walk with his heavy rolling gait toward his own quarters while Fritzche turned his attention to guiding the U-214 toward her home berth. Above them everywhere it continued, this eruption of horrors.

2

HEINRICH STEIN GLANCED at his radium-dial watch. It was nearly nine o'clock. He sat up in the darkness of the room he had rented in the tiny lodge at Freiburg, near the Swiss border.

He turned on the electric light and glanced at the door, assuring himself it was locked. He walked to the bureau, where a basin and pitcher of water had been placed by the innkeeper's buxom daughter. Stein rinsed his face off and dried it, glancing again at his watch. Where was Johann?

He walked to the bed, got down on hands and knees, and dragged the battered suitcase from underneath. With a sigh, he placed it on the bed and lifted his bulk upright. He unstrapped the suitcase and looked inside. There were twenty thousand Swiss francs, ten thousand American dollars, and five thousand English pounds, all in neat rows.

Stein reached into the suitcase and removed the Walther 9mm. pistol. His official identification was also in the suitcase. Now he took his papers and placed them inside his coat pocket. He strapped the suitcase shut and went out onto the balcony to look across the border at the Alps, stark and limitless against the black, starry night. The wind was cold across the snowy valley.

A knock sounded at the door, furtive and faint.

"About time," Stein muttered, going across the room. He opened the door to find his Swiss guide before him. "Where have you been, Johann, I've got to get back . . ." Then he noticed, simultaneously, the dismay on Johann's face and the two bulky men in gray overcoats behind him.

"Oh God, Gestapo," he moaned.

He was jerked forward by his shirt front, knocked back by

a meaty fist slamming into the side of his face. He had a brief glimpse of the innkeeper's astonished daughter peering at him before the door was slammed shut and the Gestapo really got to work.

In Berlin, the big, nondescript man paced up and down behind the blinding lights. Stein was sitting in a wooden chair, his hands taped to the arms, his feet to the legs. He had ridden through the night, similarly bound, in the backseat of a Gestapo Mercedes-Benz. Each time he had moved or groaned, they had kicked him. One man had sat over him burning his exposed flesh with the glowing tip of his cigarettes. Now all of that had stopped. The big man simply paced back and forth.

"You know you will die."

"Yes."

"Do you want to die, Stein? Why would you wish to die? For what reason? Are you a Jew-lover?"

"No. It was for the money."

"It was for the money that you transported foreign currency to Switzerland for a cell of Jews." The man's voice had grown mild. He had temporarily stopped pacing. "Answer me, Stein!"

"Yes," Stein said miserably. His head sunk slowly forward until his chin was on his chest, but a hand grabbed his thinning hair from behind and jerked his head upright again.

"Abwehr," the man behind the lights said. "You are an Abwehr agent. Answer, please, Stein!"

"Yes. I am Abwehr."

"What else have you given to these Jews, Stein? Perhaps intelligence information, perhaps the Abwehr codes!" The man leaned forward, and Stein caught a glimpse of his harsh, pitted face.

"Of course not," Stein said. A fist slammed into the back of his skull, and silver pinwheels started spinning behind his eyes. Pain shot up his spine.

"You are a traitor, Stein, do you know what that means?" his interrogator asked, beginning his pacing once more.

"I believe so," Stein said with some difficulty. His mouth

was filled with blood, his tongue was thick. He could feel the sharp edges of his broken front teeth. The room was cold, damp. Stein had fouled his pants; he stank.

"Do you know what it means to the family of one who had turned his back on the Fatherland?"

Stein's heart began to pound wildly against his rib cage. His eyes were riveted on the shadowy Gestapo agent.

Eva. A sudden, sharp image of his young wife appeared in his tortured mind. Eva and five-year-old Klaus, bright-eyed, eager Klaus. Stein had a tactile memory of the boy's chubby, tanned arms going around his neck as he leaped into his homecoming father's arms, his legs wrapping tightly around Stein's waist, his play-smudged face beaming.

"What do you want?" Stein asked miserably.

"Everything."

An hour later the Gestapo colonel, whose name was Weidling, sat in his office smoking a Russian cigarette, reading the report on the Interrogation of Heinrich Stein. He is actually smiling, thought Weidling's aide.

"I can't credit all of that, can you, Colonel Weidling?"

"It doesn't matter if it's all true or not. There is some substance. The Führer will be pleased; Field Marshal Goering will be pleased. And that should please you, Weizmann."

"Yes, Herr Colonel." Weizmann paused. "Shall I send a courier?"

"No." Weidling rose heavily. "I will hand-deliver it. It is the bad news I send by courier, Weizmann, only the bad news."

"You were right. Right all along! Who are these traitors? I want them killed. No, I want them to have a public trial first. I want them humiliated, and then I want them killed! Did you see the names of those implicated! Dr. Mueller. Colonel Oster!" The little man with the toothbrush mustache hurled Weidling's report the length of the table, and the corpulent field marshal grunted as he stretched out a red hand and picked it up.

Hitler paced before the huge, arched window of his Berchtesgaden retreat. Below, the snowy mountains stretched out toward the pale blue horizon.

Goering looked again at the report. Heinrich Stein, an Abwehr agent captured trafficking with Jews, had implicated Colonel Oster and a dozen other Abwehr officers in a plot to kill Adolf Hitler. Substantiating evidence was trickling in as suspects were subjected to "deep interrogation." There had already been three confessions. A Dr. Josef Mueller had tried to contact the British through the Vatican in 1940 to discover what peace terms would be offered if the Führer were "displaced." A man named Pastor Bonhoeffer had performed a similar traitorous act in 1942, visiting the Bishop of Chichester in Stockholm. He had traveled on a false passport issued by the Abwehr. Hans von Dohnanyi, another Abwehr agent, had been implicated in at least three failed assassination attempts and had also contacted the enemy.

"It is a rotten tree, the Abwehr," the Führer of the Third Reich said at last. "I should have listened when you told me that you wished to absorb it into Himmler's RSHA. How can I trust any of these military leaders! They have shown their cowardice on both fronts—retreating when only attack can gain us victory!" Hitler's eyes were closed, his right fist tightly clenched, his head thrown back so that the tendons on his neck stood out. "And now this! Summon Admiral Canaris. Inform him that as of now the Abwehr is dissolved! Inform Himmler that the SD is to assume all former Abwehr functions."

"Yes, my Führer."

"And tell him to dig deeply. Comb the Abwehr records. There are more traitors we have not uncovered, Hermann. More plots. More who would sell us out to the English, more men who have given us false information allowing our enemies to gain the upper hand!" Hitler's lips were flecked with foam now as he walked to the head of the table and braced himself against it with his clenched hands. "They must be rooted out to the last man. And killed. I will not suffer them to live, Hermann."

*   *   *

15

"Well," Albert Bruckman said loudly, "that's it, I suppose."

August Diels looked up from his Baltic reports curiously. "What, Albert?"

"You haven't heard?"

"Heard what, for God's sake! Is the war over?"

"Ours is," Bruckman said, leaning back in his chair, steepling his fingers.

"I don't know what you're talking about, Bruckman. I really haven't got time for riddles just now."

"Where the hell have you been, Diels?"

"Been when? This morning? At the chancellery. Why?" Diels felt the first tugging of apprehension. "What's happened?"

"We're out of a job. Didn't you see the SD men in the foyer? The Abwehr, my friend, has been dissolved."

"That's ludicrous!"

"No. Military intelligence," Bruckman yawned, "is now a function of the beloved Reichssicherheitshauptampt. RSHA to you."

"I can't believe it!" Diels rose out of his chair as if impelled by steel springs. "How? Why?"

"You really don't keep your ears open, do you? Remember Dohnanyi?"

"Hans? Yes, but—"

"Colonel Oster?"

"Certainly," Diels replied, his frown deepening.

"Well, it seems they had this wonderful inspiration"— Bruckman's chair snapped forward—"to kill Hitler."

"Oh, God!" Diels moaned.

"Exactly, and they've been caught. An agent named Stein, who was posted in Freiburg, was captured trying to smuggle currency to a gang of Jews in Switzerland, and when the Gestapo got their hands on him he talked. Hell, he probably made up half if it, but that won't do Oster or Dohnanyi any good. Their offices are closed up, and Admiral Canaris has been whisked away to Berchtesgaden."

"What of us?" Diels asked. His back was now turned. He stood looking morosely at the bombed city below his window.

Here and there people poked among the rubble, looking for God knows what.

"We're out," Bruckman said. "First there will be some interrogation, a scouring of our personal files, and then, if we're lucky, a trip home. Or maybe we'll all be sent to the front, I don't know."

Bruckman yawned again, wondering if Helga was on this floor and if there was time to visit the basement once more before Buehler's peopled moved in.

Diels dug something out of his desk and went out, moving very slowly. Bruckman watched him with little interest. In the corridor Diels turned to the right and shuffled toward the lavatory. SD Major Birger Buehler was striding toward him, appearing taller now, more confident. He had gotten what he wanted. Diels passed him without saying a word and went into the lavatory.

"Wasn't that Diels?" Buehler asked, pulling up abruptly.

"Yes, sir."

"Get him. I want to speak to him first. I've always thought there was something funny going on with August Diels."

The two uniformed SD men turned toward the lavatory. They had taken three steps when the gunshot rang out. Buehler pushed past his men and rushed into the lavatory. Diels was sprawled half-in, half-out of a commode booth, the muzzle of the pistol still between his teeth, the back of his head spattered all over the wall. Buehler hovered over him briefly, his mouth twitching. Then he spun on his heel and stalked out of the lavatory, pushing through the gathering crowd of Abwehr staff.

"I want that man's files gone over immediately! Every scrap of paper in his desk, at his house, in the records-department files. It is imperative."

"Yes, Major Buehler."

"Also the homes of any friends. Anyone who works in the same office."

"Yes, Herr Major."

"Immediately."

They began immediately, but the results did not cheer Buehler. There was nothing at all out of order in Diels's Baltic reports, and although his flat was torn apart board by board, there was nothing found to implicate Diels in passing intelligence to the enemy or in plotting with other Abwehr men to assassinate the Führer. It was not until they had finished Diels's files and started in on those of his associates that anything came to light.

"There are documents missing, Major."

Bruckman's files were arranged in neat stacks on the major's desk. "How do we know this?" he asked, picking one at random and thumbing through it.

"Bruckman himself admits that there are reports missing, but he claims to have no knowledge of why. He does not know, he says, when or how they could have been taken."

"It would be very simple for a man in his office, I would think."

"These are only concentration-camp reports, Herr Major. What use are they to anyone? How could they have been taken out anyway? Abwehr internal security was fairly strict."

"It shouldn't have been difficult," Buehler said. His mind, however, was on the lieutenant's first question—of what use were they? The answer was evident and appalling. Time was winding down. The Third Reich was dying. American and British armies had crossed the English Channel and were storming through France; Rommel and von Rundstedt were reeling before the advance. Naval superiority had never existed, and Goering's vaunted Luftwaffe was no longer in control of the skies. One had only to look out the window to see that. This city and others lay in ruins.

The war was lost, and after the war would come the tribunals. Buehler got up slowly. "I must see Himmler. Have a report written up right away."

"Yes, Major."

"I only wonder where Diels sent those documents. If they are in Allied hands already, it is hopeless, of course. But perhaps they are still in Germany."

"There was the father, sir," the lieutenant reminded him.

"Of course! His father is Abwehr."

"However, we dismissed that as an improbability considering the elder Diels's situation. After all," the lieutenant laughed, "Africa . . . !"

Buehler, however, was not laughing as he went out the door, tugging his cap on. The lieutenant shrugged and began picking up the folders. He barely had time to collect them when the air-raid sirens sounded. He dashed toward the basement, the folders under one arm.

3

THE LITTLE MAN was in a rage. He kicked over a heavy wooden chair and struck himself on the forehead three times in a row. Heinrich Himmler sat staring at him. There was nothing to say, nothing to do. The man's universe was collapsing.

"Abwehr," the Führer said eventually.

"Yes."

"I thought I ordered them executed. All of them."

"This man," Himmler said patiently, "was not implicated in the attempts on your life. The other matter only came to light after he had died of his own hand."

"Diels." The Führer stood looking out the window at the heavy rain. "That was his name."

"Yes."

"Why, Heinrich? Are they not good Germans, these men?"

Himmler didn't answer. There wasn't any point.

The Führer turned to face him. "He had the authorization papers?"

"Yes," Himmler answered. "The papers signed by your hand. Countersigned by mine," he added.

That was not important to the Führer. Only his own role in the extermination camps, the medical experiments, the final solution, only his own image, his stature in history.

"Those papers must not exist," the small man said, exploding with fresh fury. He began stalking, his hands forming choppy, uncontrolled gestures. "They *must not* exist. I will not accept the responsibility for this. Where are they now?"

"Africa," Himmler said, and the Führer turned toward him, his face wooden.

"Africa?" Hitler repeated.

"This Diels, he has a father, also Abwehr, stationed in the Cameroons. Apparently, he has been sending his father papers stolen from his superiors' files. A man in Diels's office, an Albert Bruckman, indicates that he knew about this."

"But he did not report it!"

"It seems Bruckman was involved in certain illicit activities that Diels knew about. Bruckman was afraid of being prosecuted."

"He did not report it!" Hitler repeated. What sort of men were these? What sort of Nazis, what sort of Germans, to see traitors at work and let them operate beneath their noses? "Bruckman is dead?"

"Of course."

Hitler rocked on the balls of his feet. His temper seemed to have subsided, but it was always there, simmering beneath the surface.

"I want a trustworthy SD man sent to the Cameroons immediately. The papers must be found, Heinrich. I will not tolerate it! I was a fool to allow myself to be badgered into signing them."

That wasn't at all the way Himmler recalled it happening, but again he said nothing. The Führer had begun to pace. "Have we an airfield there?"

"No longer. Enemy operatives have destroyed it."

"Destroyed it." The Führer looked at Himmler as if that, too, were part of a conspiracy.

"May I make a suggestion, sir?" Himmler said softly. "The chances of an aircarft making such a long flight are at present very slim. There may or may not be landing fields; there may or may not be fuel to be found. There is a virtual net of enemy fighters to be gotten through."

"Yes, the suggestion, Heinrich!"

"A submarine."

"A submarine? No. We need our U-boats. They are our backbone."

Not anymore, Himmler thought but did not say—not with the enemy rolling across France. Still, he knew the Führer's feeling about the U-boat service. They were the loyal ones, the invincible force.

"There is a submarine scheduled to depart for African waters at this moment, mein Führer. I have already looked into this. A long-range submarine captained by one of our finest, most loyal officers. His mission was disruption of Allied shipping lanes to North Africa. With a slight change in his orders, this most important business with the disloyal Abwehr man can be included in his mission."

"I want SS men on board."

"Of course."

"I want this Abwehr traitor killed!"

"Yes, mein Führer."

"And the papers—Heinrich, I will have those papers. The world must never know that Adolf Hitler personally executed an order for the final solution."

The black Stuka cut its superchargers and started its descent toward the badly cratered airfield at Wilhemshaven. The control tower had been reduced to rubble. The sea looked dark and ominous beneath the rolling gray skies.

"Captain von Roenne!" someone was calling before the pilot had even killed the engines. Von Roenne, who was unfastening his parachute—which he wouldn't have known how to work— leaned out of the aircraft and shouted an answer.

"The car is waiting, sir," the soldier said, extremely nervous. "We're already quite late. Colonel Olbricht is waiting!" He shouted above the whine of the dying engines.

The ladder was dropped over and von Roenne climbed down, catching his bag, which the pilot had thrown down before touching his cap in a farewell salute.

Von Roenne ducked low and followed the soldier across the pitted field to the waiting car.

"Who in hell is Colonel Olbricht?" the count asked as he climbed into the backseat and slammed the door.

"SD, sir. Colonel Georg Olbricht. He's said to be very close to Himmler."

"Small distinction," von Roenne muttered as the car lurched forward with a squeal of rubber.

What, he wondered, does the SD have to do with submarine service? He had no liking for the SD, the SS, the Gestapo— all of those "civilian soldiers" who had never and would never face an armed enemy, who rose through their top-heavy ranks in direct proportion to the servility they displayed toward their superiors. Von Roenne leaned back in the seat, watching as the car roared down the empty streets of the once-pleasant seaport and made for the submarine pens.

The car passed through a succession of guarded gates and headed to the long reinforced concrete quay, which also showed signs of aerial attack. As the car stopped, von Roenne saw a lumbering figure approach. There was something familiar about this sailor, who, though the wind off the sea was cold, wore a short-sleeved undershirt that exposed massive, ornately tattooed arms.

"Rudi!" Von Roenne strode toward Rudi Johst. The chief engineer grinned broadly, revealing a gap where his front teeth had been. Johst halted, heels together, saluted, and then took von Roenne's hand in a warm, iron-firm clasp. "You're going to be with me?" Roenne asked, stepping back, still holding Johst's hand.

"All of the old crew, sir. We're all here. Fritzche, Renhardt, old Stutters . . . All except Eisner. His house was hit while he was home on leave. His wife and all five kids, too. Damned shame."

"Damned shame," von Roenne agreed. To have come through as much as they all had, then to be struck by mindless bombs falling blindly from the skies. . . .

"The colonel is waiting, sir," the driver said shakily.

"Nervous one, ain't he?" Johst asked. He laughed. "We're at the end of the quay, sir. The old one-ninety-one, it is. I've got her running proper now, though."

"One-ninety-one?" That had been Lieutenant Holzlohner's boat. Von Roenne had gone through the naval academy with Holzlohner.

23

"Hadn't you heard, sir?" Johst said heavily. His eyes flickered toward the buildings beyond von Roenne's shoulder, and his voice lowered still more. "They arrested him for cowardice."

"Who did!" von Roenne exploded. "Holzlohner a coward? Ridiculous. What happened?"

"It's a tale for later, sir," Johst said, inclining his head toward the driver.

"All right," said the count, taking a slow deep breath of the icy air. He looked toward the white-flecked gray sea beyond the quay and told Johst, "I'll be along. Have a bottle anywhere?"

"Always, sir. Scotch whisky too, the real thing, prize of war."

"Sir?" the driver croaked.

"All right. All right, I'll see this Colonel Olbricht. Lead the way."

Von Roenne was led through a high gate and up to a dilapidated green frame building. The glass had been blown out of every window, the front door recently replaced.

Inside, they passed a reception desk manned by a narrow, red-headed sergeant. "This way, sir." They continued to a flight of stairs that led to the second story. The bombed base headquarters smelled like a very old house, long-empty, von Roenne noticed. "Watch your step, please, sir," the driver said.

There was a huge splintered hole in the floor, boarded over carelessly with used lumber. Von Roenne looked up to see that the roof, too, had been hastily patched.

"It came right on through," the soldier informed him. "A hundred-pounder. A dud. They defused it and left it in the basement."

The open door led into the base commander's office. Admiral Kapp was there, looking old and weary in his new uniform. He was a big pink and white man with a Kaiser mustache and tiny eyes. Beside him was Admiral Popitz, the commander of the Seventh Flotilla, only a fragment of which still existed. And behind the desk sat an SD officer.

"Good afternoon, von Roenne," Kapp said as Roenne saluted both officers and shook their hands.

"It looks as if it's been a little rugged around here," the count said.

"Not good," Kapp admitted, looking slightly worried, like a man who has forgotten his wife's shopping list.

"If you gentlemen will leave me alone with Captain von Roenne," the SD man said, rising.

"Of course." Kapp looked startled. But then he wasn't used to being ordered from his own office. The two admirals went out, and a black-uniformed SS man, who had appeared from nowhere, leaned in and pulled the door shut. Von Roenne was left alone with the SD colonel.

"Sit down, Captain von Roenne. Let me introduce myself. I am Colonel Georg Olbricht of the *Sicherheitsdienst*." Roenne, who had slacked into a chair and taken his enameled cigarette case from an inside pocket, lit the cigarette in his mouth, nodded, and blew the smoke away from before his ravaged yet still-handsome face.

"And what is it that you wished to see me about, Herr Colonel? A submarine assignment, of course, and something in the more secretive line or the SD would not be involved."

Olbricht, von Roenne noted, was no longer attempting that grotesque smile. His florid face was set, and his jowls wagged a little as he shook his head. The oddly wet eyes that flanked his small nose fixed themselves on the count. Von Roenne could not guess at the colonel's thoughts and had no desire to try.

"You would make a detective," Olbricht said, trying to be hearty. Von Roenne just shrugged again. "There is a very special mission that must be undertaken. It must be done by submarine."

"Of course." Since that was virtually the only German vessel offering any sort of security on the high seas.

"This mission originates in the highest echelon," Olbricht said. He took a sealed yellow envelope from his coat pocket and tossed it onto the desk near von Roenne's elbow. "When you see the signature of those orders, you will understand the interest the highest levels of government are taking in this."

Von Roenne didn't lift a finger to examine the envelope or its enclosed orders. Olbricht's jaw twitched, and the damp, dark eyes narrowed. "You seem bored, *Count* von Roenne; I hope I am not boring you."

"No," von Roenne said after a pause. "Let me explain myself, Olbricht. I am a warrior. I haven't the slightest interest in the origin of orders—indeed, in the point of this mission—unless it affects my ability to perform my duties. I need to know only two things from you—where we are going and when you wish to leave."

"I see." Olbricht's voice was a hiss. Von Roenne stubbed out his cigarette and watched without expression as the veil of smoke lifted from between their eyes. "Very well," the SD colonel went on brusquely, "your vessel is the U-191. You are completely familiar with this submarine type?"

Roenne smiled with faint amusement. "The U-191, unless it has been recently modified, is a typical Type Seven-C Unterseeboot. It is two hundred twenty and one-quarter feet long and displaces seven hundred sixty-nine tons submerged. Its surface speed is seventeen knots, its underwater speed seven and a half knots. It carries a crew of forty-four and is armed with five torpedo tubes, four forward, one aft. It also has a three-point-five-inch deck gun. It can travel slightly under twenty-four hours submerged, using battery power which reduces the speed to only four knots. However, its range is an incomparable sixty-five hundred miles. Its steering system—"

"I am convinced that you attended naval college," Olbricht said sharply. Von Roenne reached for another cigarette, fumbling for it with his damaged hand. "Perhaps I asked what you considered to be a stupid question, but I am not a naval man."

Nor a soldier, von Roenne thought but did not say. He lit his cigarette.

"It is, at any rate," Colonel Olbricht continued, "the last point in your dissertation which interests us chiefly. That is to say, the remarkable range of the Type Seven submarine. Have you had occasion to test this?"

"I made two runs to Nova Scotia back in 'forty-two. Sixteen kills on those runs."

"Then a long-range operation is nothing new to you."

"Colonel, nothing about a submarine is new to me. We are intimate to the extreme after five years of this. Ashore, I dream of my submarine and not of beautiful women." Olbricht coughed a small laugh.

"Very good. And so—tell me this—have you heard of the Cameroons?"

"Vaguely. In Africa, yes?"

"Yes. What we need to know is this—can you take me and my people there?"

"If you have the charts, I can take you anywhere—assuming we aren't sunk en route, that is. It's more than a little hazardous out there just now. We have to count on a little luck."

"You have this luck."

"Some say I do." Roenne turned his hand over, examining it. "And some say that I do not."

"And you are without a doubt the most skilled submarine commander still alive."

"Oh," von Roenne agreed, "without a doubt, Colonel Olbricht. The Cameroons, is it? I shall have to look that up. You have collected my regular crew for me, I have discovered. That will make this all the easier. It's essential to have men with you that you know on a submarine, especially when things get tight."

"So I was given to understand. By the way, you will notice some modifications. Twenty extra bunks have been added. It is necessary for me to take some SS personnel with me."

Von Roenne only nodded. He rose and said, "I had better get on down and see how things stand. When do we leave?"

"At eighteen hundred hours."

"So soon? Well, that's all right too. Maybe we'll be out of the pens before the next wave of bombers come across." He had started toward the door when he paused and asked without turning his head, "By the way, the one-ninety-one was Lieutenant Holzlohner's vessel. Why wasn't he given this assignment?"

"It is my understanding that Lieutenant Holzlohner has been relieved of duty."

"Oh? May I ask why?"

"His nerves, I believe. Shot to pieces." Then von Roenne did glance across his shoulder, and he surprised Olbricht with the smile on his face. It was a vicious, brutal expression, which vanished as the count's eyes met those of the SD colonel.

"Good day, then," von Roenne said. "Make sure I get those charts, all right?"

Then he opened the door and stepped out past the SS man, who stood, hands behind his back, staring past the naval officer. Von Roenne turned and started up the bomb-torn corridor, his right foot dragging slightly from the old injury, his thoughts far away, not on the Cameroons and Olbricht's mysterious and important mission, but on Karl Holzlohner, a small, private man with flaming red hair, a quick grin, and a mountain of courage for a heart.

"Good day, sir!" Seaman Best was on watch at the submarine's boarding plank, wearing a white helmet and armed with a Mauser and ammunition belt. His enthusiasm at seeing von Roenne was apparent. The captain saluted sharply, then shook Horst's hand. What von Roenne had told Olbricht was absolutely true. The crew of a submarine has to be close, and von Roenne, who was a god on earth to some of his men, enforced his peculiar iron rule by earning the right to their devotion, not by threatening them. There was no room for that sort of rule on a U-boat, and anyway, despite his aristocratic origins, Roenne was not inclined toward such behavior. The knights of Baden-Württemberg would be turning in their graves again, von Roenne thought as he slapped Best on the shoulder and walked aboard the U-191, pausing with his hand on the rail of the gangway to look up at the shifting low clouds, then across the submarine pens at the rusted and wrecked vessels that the pens had not saved.

"Welcome aboard, sir," said Rudi Johst.

Von Roenne handed the sailor his seabag. "Everything all right, Rudi?"

"Great shape. They pulled the bearings, and everything is like new."

"Fine. What are we carrying for weaponry? Mines or torpedoes?"

"Torpedoes," Johst said as they walked forward, their shoes ringing on the wooden catwalks laid over the steel deck of the U-191.

"Any of our visitors aboard?"

"If you mean those bastard SS men, yes. Almost all of them. I've been moved out, and so have Heillman and Krueger. They cut the galley in half and emptied out the aft torpedo compartment to sling some hammocks. Guess who gets those accommodations?"

Von Roenne smiled. He didn't have to guess. "I'll try to straighten it out. I'll explain to Olbricht that I need my men in their accustomed places, so that there's no confusion when we sound battle stations. After all, the SS men aren't going to do anything when the klaxon sounds but sit around and sweat."

"I don't see that damned Olbricht caring about it." They had started down the forward hatch, von Roenne in the lead, going cautiously, his arm hooked around the ladder to give him a grip he couldn't manage with his misshapen hand. He waited for Johst at the foot of the ladder, and they walked single-file toward the captain's quarters.

Von Roenne tossed his satchel on the bunk and looked around at what had once been Holzlohner's cabin.

"Sit down, Rudi," the captain said. He lifted his chin toward the oval-shaped watertight cabin door, and Johst closed it. He seated himself at the steel table opposite von Roenne, who sat on the bunk and lit a cigarette.

"What happened to Karl Holzlohner?"

"I just know what I've heard from the SS," Johst said, folding his huge arms across his chest. He clenched his fists as he spoke so that the girl on either forearm danced before von Roenne's eyes. "They know because Olbricht bragged about it to them."

"What does Colonel Olbricht have to do with it?"

"He was on the *Volksgerichtshof*, sir. He watched Lieutenant Holzlohner go down."

"I don't understand you," von Roenne said, shaking his head vigorously. "You mean Holzlohner was dragged before a people's court? That's a civilian organ; they can't try a military man."

"They tried Field Marshal von Witzleben, sir, and General Hoepner. *And* General Stieff, and General von Hase. Hitler swore that the Wehrmacht tried to assassinate him—and who knows? Maybe they found the guts to try."

"Yes, I remember it all now. I liked von Hase. But how in hell did Holzlohner get involved in something like that?"

"The Abwehr thing, sir. I wonder why this nation can't produce a good assassin. They keep fumbling it."

"Holzlohner was a man like myself, Johst. He could no more turn his back on the oaths he's taken than I could. He was not involved in any sort of plot—I know this without hearing any evidence!"

"No, sir, he wasn't."

"Then what . . . ?"

"But he knew something. He knew something and he didn't report it. A cousin of his—Gunther Fricke I believe was his name—was Abwehr. He got drunk at a party one night and told Holzlohner that certain people were going to take care of that lunatic Hitler."

"And someone else overheard."

"Gestapo. They didn't pull them in just them. They waited, and when this Abwher thing finally blew, Fricke and Holzlohner were netted with the rest of them."

"But surely there wasn't enough against Karl to justify relieving him of command."

"Oh, there was by then. It seems one of his crew turned against him after spending the night in a basement with some Getapo thugs. It was the chief torpedo man, can't recall his name. He told the court that the one-ninety-one failed to en-

30

gage the enemy returning from the Mediterranean. What it was, sir, was a convoy of six destroyers. Holzlohner had two torpedoes—it was only prudent to go down to a hundred fathoms and wait for them to pass. Which is exactly what they did."

"Where is he?" von Roenne said vehemently, rising. "Where is Holzlohner now? Maybe we can do something."

"No, sir," Johst said, looking at the dancing girls and not at his captain. "There's nothing to be done. They took him into a shed next to the courthouse and garotted him, hung him up on a hook to rot. He's dead, sir," Johst said, raising his eyes at last.

A full minute passed during which it seemed to Johst that Peter Karl Neff, Count von Roenne, did not even breathe. He simply stood looking at the steel bulkhead of the U-191, biting his upper lip.

"All right, Rudi," he said at last. "Thank you for telling me. I wouldn't speak of it to anyone else, however. We get underway at eighteen hundred hours. Find Lieutenant Fritzche, please, and have him meet me on the bridge."

"Very good, sir," Johst said. He started to salute, hesitated, then spun sharply on his heel and went out, leaving von Roenne to stand staring at the open doorway.

4

It was already dark at eighteen hundred hours. The sea was rising, the skies groaning, the wind brisk from the northeast. Colonel Olbricht strode down the quay with two uniformed SS men beside him. He looked uneasily at the bay, the Jade Busen. He saw the ravaged submarine pens, the menacing silhouette of the awaiting U-191. He had mentioned to no one that this was his first time aboard a seagoing vessel. And it had to be a submarine! Locked in the damned thing like the dead in an iron casket.

The salt air was crisp, the wind bitter against his florid face. "It has to be done," he told himself as he and the SS man went aboard. The orders had come from the very top. He could hear the diesel engines burbling throatily below the waterline.

He went down the hatch, followed by his soldiers. The lights from below seemed too dim, otherworldly. When the hatch clanged shut above him, the echoes reverberated through the submarine. Olbricht felt chilled.

He worked his way forward, still with his two lieutenants at his shoulders. Erzberger, the taller of the men, the fair-haired one, was silent. His eyes were blue and emotionless. Not Ziegler's. Ziegler's were never emotionless, although the man was utterly self-controlled. He could check his violent temper, hold it in until ordered to kill.

Ulrich Ziegler was the son of a glassblower, although he pretended that his people had been landholders in Bavaria. He had been thrown out of every school he attended, usually for beating other students—and twice, his teachers. In Düsseldorf he attempted to burn down the trade school. One teacher had taken it on himself to straighten Ulrich Ziegler out. With a rod.

Ziegler had been unable to walk for a week after the beating, and he had changed. But the eyes still simmered; they were always alive in the head of this huge, blocky man with the close-cropped dark hair, the scarred chin.

They found Captain von Roenne forward, giving orders to the eight sailors and officers around him. His eyes flickered toward the hatch as Olbricht and his SS men entered the control room.

"Get those people out of here," von Roenne told Olbricht. Olbricht saw Ziegler stiffen. These days people didn't tell an SS officer what to do. "They're to stay in their quarters, do you understand that?"

"Yes, Captain von Roenne," the colonel answered with some sarcasm, which the count ignored. Olbricht inclined his head, and the two black-clad SS officers left, Ziegler glancing back, his eyes full of fire.

As soon as the pens were cleared, von Roenne went to periscope depth. A squadron of B-24s had been spotted earlier in the day, and there was every chance that British warships were on patrol nearby. The Allies were determined to throttle what remained of the U-boat menace, and Wilhelmshaven was a primary target. The Allies couldn't know how close to being crippled Wilhelmshaven was. The bottom of the harbor was littered with the hulks of submarines—and their trapped crews. The great iron net that had once screened the harbor from underwater attack no longer stood guard.

"You will have to circle the British Islands?" Olbricht asked. In the greenish light cast by the instrument, he watched von Roenne's face.

"Through the English Channel," von Roenne replied.

"The Channel! Surely that's impossible."

Roenne shrugged. "Maybe. It gets us through enemy waters more quickly than if we circle England and Ireland."

"But it seems to me—"

"Colonel, I don't care much how it seems to you. This is my vessel, and even in the Third Reich the captain has complete authority at sea."

Olbricht swallowed his rejoinder. He stood aside, listening to the quietly spoken orders, the humming of the electrical motors, the pings and beeps he did not understand, the thrumming of the diesel engines. After half an hour he went to his own quarters, lay down on the bunk and listened to submarine groans and creaks. He tried to sleep but couldn't. His mind was on the crushing mass of sea beyond the ship's thin skin. His heart raced as he lay there, the sweat trickling from his brow, the strange sounds of the undersea vessel rumbling in his ears.

Hours later he was still there, turning from side to side, his nostrils filled with the damp iron and oil smells of the U-191. He rolled onto his side and then returned to his back, flinging his forearm across his eyes. Nothing helped. He wondered if he would be able to sleep at all this trip.

Certainly. One grows used to anything. That thought nestled comfortingly in his consciousness and had begun to spread soft, soothing wings across his anxiety when the klaxon sounded— a loud, metallic sound that brought Olbricht to his feet at once. He felt the submarine shift beneath his feet. Felt the deck tilt and seem to fall away ever so slightly. Outside his cabin, seamen rushed past. He flung open the door and went out, making his way forward, jostled by intent sailors.

Ziegler and Erzberger were standing near the galley, looking back and forth in confusion.

"What is this, Herr Colonel?" Erzberger asked, but Olbricht simply pushed past them.

He found von Roenne with headphones on, listening intently to the sharp ring of the asdic/sonar, peering at the green scope around which a sweep hand moved. Seen in that light, his face was utterly placid, both old and young—pleased, Olbricht thought, devilishly pleased.

"What is it?" Olbricht asked, tapping von Roenne's shoulder. Von Roenne turned, lifting one earpiece. "I said, what is it, Captain?"

"A convoy, Colonel Olbricht. Perhaps a dozen ships. Undoubtedly troop carriers. Destroyers flanking."

"What in God's name has that to do with us!" Olbricht exploded. A bit of perspiration broke free of his eyebrow and tracked down into his eye, stinging it. He wiped it away in annoyance. "Have they discovered us?"

"No." Von Roenne turned away. "Activate TDC, Best. Fritzche, arm forward torpedo tubes, stand by."

"What are you doing!" Olbricht's hand stretched out and clutched von Roenne's shoulder. Von Roenne turned coldly toward the SD colonel and told him quietly, "I am attacking, sir. It is my duty."

"Not now. With us on board? Jeopardizing this mission!"

"These are targets of opportunity," the captain replied. "What am I to do? Turn my back on my duty?"

"They've heard us, sir," Best said. Von Roenne listened intently through his headphones and nodded.

"Two, possibly three. Ready torpedo tubes for firing. On my mark."

"Are you insane?" Olbricht shrieked. He spun von Roenne around. Olbricht's face was glossed with perspiration—the perspiration of fear and anxiety. "Can't you understand that my mission comes first?"

"It is my duty," von Roenne said, and Olbricht saw the corner of his mouth hook up with what might have been amusement. "I am not a coward, after all."

"No one thinks you are, von Roenne, for God's sake!"

"Five hundred meters, sir."

"It might be said that I am if I fail to attack." The dart struck home. Olbricht knew suddenly what he was talking about. He stepped back and stood, fists opening and closing, his tongue waving about in his dry mouth.

"Three hundred."

"Up periscope and stand by to mark."

"Von Roenne!"

"Two hundred."

"Are you ordering me to break off, Colonel?" the captain asked carefully.

"Yes, damn it. Yes, I am."

Von Roenne stood with his shoulder against the scope tube, his arms crossed, his pale eyes fixed on Olbricht. Slowly he nodded. "Dive! Evasive action. Take us to a hundred meters."

Olbricht stood frozen, listening to the ping of the asdic, watching the scope nearby as the submarine went down at an acute angle. He heard a nearby, nearly inaudible click and then the muffled boom of a depth charge. The 191 swayed violently, and Olbricht glanced anxiously at von Roenne, who was casually lighting a cigarette. Another depth charge, more distant, exploded, and another, but the 191 was running deep and silent by now, and they knew the destroyers had lost her.

Olbricht walked away, moving very slowly, his footsteps muffled.

"Sir?" Lieutenant Fritzche was beside Roenne, who just stood there, smoking nonchalantly.

"Keep her at a hundred meters for half an hour, Fritzche. Then bring her up to thirty if asdic contact is negative. At midnight we'll go up and run on the surface to keep the speed up. I want to get Olbricht and his people to their destination as quickly as possible."

"Yes, sir. Captain—he won't forget that."

"No," von Roenne said. "I don't intend that he should."

"Shut up, for Christ's sake!" Eric O'Reilley shouted. His voice echoed eerily through the stone corridors.

"That won't do any good, O'Reilley," Becque said with a chuckle. "You have to put up with Bombo when you're naughty."

O'Reilley glowered at the Frenchman, though it was doubtful Becque could see the expression in the darkness of the prison. Becque walked slowly away from the iron-barred cell door, holding the key ring behind his back. O'Reilley settled back against the gray stone wall, glancing once at the other man in the cell.

Down the corridor Bombo, who had gotten drunk on white liquor and killed a tribesman, continued his moaning: a ululating, heart-rending sound that continued day and night in Victoria Prison, British Cameroons. O'Reilley mopped his perspiring forehead with the sleeve of his shirt.

"Poor devil," Kruger said. The South African was crouched in the corner, idly sifting straw through his fingers. Through a high, narrow window—the only source of fresh air and illumination in Victoria Prison—shone the last purple light of day.

Bombo did not understand. Bombo was Bamileke, and he lived by the laws of his people, doing what must be done. A man had stepped on the grave of his father, so Bombo had killed him. That was the law. It was necessary. But the French had locked him up.

For two years Bombo had chipped away at the stone wall of his cell with a smuggled bit of steel. He had dug out a crater the size of his head. Then the French had discovered the hole and had moved Bombo to another cell. There he sat, wailing, praying, singing his despair.

Becque was returning slowly, pacing the corridor. The jailer was a French legionnaire who had come down from N'Djamena with the rest of them when that puppet Brieux had been ordered to retake British Cameroons for his German masters.

The battle for Douala, the chief Cameroons port, had been bloodless. Major Pierre Brieux had simply presented himself at the British governor's house and informed him that the Vichy French forces were seizing all of the Cameroons for the Germans, who had originally claimed the African territory in 1884. The British governor, Lord Harold Gore, had taken the civilized approach of inviting Brieux into his house for a glass of claret.

"How's your head now?" Becque asked in French, leaning his forehead against the bars to peer in.

"Not too bad."

"That rum," Becque laughed. "Very rough stuff."

"So's a truncheon," O'Reilley answered, and Becque laughed again.

"We can't have people destroying our only cabaret, O'Reilley."

"So the judge said."

"One more night. You'll be out tomorrow. Then what? Back to the hunting?"

"Back to the cabaret," O'Reilley answered. "And the next Frog that tries to knock my head off with a nightstick is going to get a big surprise."

"You are incorrigible, O'Reilley. I think one day it will be as it is with Bombo for you." There with a hint of something sterner beneath the jailer's light tone. O'Reilley muttered a reply, and Becque strolled away again, whistling.

"What do you think?" Paul Kruger asked the American. "What do we do tomorrow night?"

"Back to the cabaret, Paul."

The South African looked at his friend, seeing only the vague oval of his face, the square shoulders encased in O'Reilley's white shirt. In another minute, as the twilight faded, Kruger could not even see that much. Yet sitting there, listening to a rat scuttle across the floor, he could feel the presence of O'Reilley, the intensity of the man, the controlled violence.

"Whatever you say, Eric. We will do it your way."

Morning brought Becque back. They heard the slow shuffling of his boots, the rattle of the key ring as he opened the cell door.

"Come on, men. Time's up."

O'Reilley rose lazily from the floor and stood, brushing the straw from his khaki pants, his white shirt, still torn and bloodied from the brawl in the Europa Cabaret. Becque looked him up and down. Hunters—that's what O'Reilley and Kruger were. Ivory, mostly—or so they said, even though elephants were now protected. This *had* been what they did. Now ships no longer came to Douala, hence there was no way to send ivory, furs, and trophy heads out of the Cameroons. O'Reilley was stranded here with the rest of them. The war, Becque supposed,

38

had brought life to a standstill in many places around the globe, but nowhere could things have come to the complete halt they had in the Cameroons.

Nothing came in, nothing left. The people who had been here in 'forty-two were still here, whether they wished to be or not. The only alternative was a thousand-mile trek to an open port like Gaba, but even if that were possible, which it wasn't, there would be no ships out.

From the Cameroons, no roads led anywhere, and the few existing tracks were in ill repair and well guarded. No one had a vehicle, no one had any fuel—when was the last time a gasoline shipment had come to Douala? And so they sat, one and all: the French, who were occupying the country; the handful of Germans, who were nominally their masters; the British; and the foreigners, who, like O'Reilley and Kruger, had nothing to do but drink local rum and wait until their fates were determined by events halfway around the world.

"Come on, Kruger. I haven't got all day."

The tall, blond South African had been standing, forming his hat to his own precise specifications. Now he put it on and walked out of the cell, following the jailer and O'Reilley, who also wore a safari hat, down the long corridor inside Victoria Prison.

"So long, Bombo," Kruger called out.

The African didn't move. He crouched in the corner of his cell, his deliberately scarred face dark and brooding, a rumbling lament rising from his throat.

"It's not doing anyone any good to hold him, you know," Kruger said.

"It's the law, Kruger," Becque answered over his shoulder.

They were passing a long row of steel-plate doors set into the stone walls of the fortress prison, and O'Reilley's eyes were moving constantly as he mapped the layout in his mind. The windows high on the wall were made from iron straps latticed to form a grill. They weren't in very good shape. The prison had been built in 1921, and the years of tropical humidity had decayed the iron bands into rust-red, corroded strips. The door to the prison kitchen stood open, and O'Reilley could see a native trusty stirring a huge iron pot with tireless rhythm. Two legionnaires stood guard in the hallway, rifles in their hands. O'Reilley glanced at Kruger, who gave no sign that anything had passed between them.

"You were lucky, really," Becque was saying. "How would you have liked to spend your time in one of these damned airless holes?" He jabbed a finger at the steel door beside him. "You think the British are a compassionate race? I ask you—"

"Almost as bad as the Bastille, eh?" O'Reilley said.

"That was long ago, Eric. Those times the aristocrats ran things. Now, since the Revolution . . ."

"Yes. You've done fine back home," O'Reilley growled.

"An Irishman who prefers the English," Becque said, shrugging his massive shoulders.

"American. And I don't prefer them."

"Good day, gentlemen. Do not return soon." They had reached the high-ceilinged foyer that led to the administration offices. O'Reilley and Kruger waited while another legionnaire unlocked the heavy oak-and-iron door and swung it open for them. Then they passed through and went to pick up their release forms and personal belongings.

"Nothing to it," Kruger said.

"Not much." O'Reilley glanced back at the cell block and nodded thoughtfully.

They did not speak again until they had collected their possessions and departed from the building. Outside it was brilliantly clear, humid as always, the sea sparkling blue beyond the row of palms along the water's edge. Bicycle traffic moved up and down the only paved road of the city.

Crossing the dead lawn before the prison, Kruger said, "I wish we could have gotten a look at him. We don't know how he's doing, what kind of shape they've left him in."

"Mesotho? Don't you worry about him, Paul. They can't break him."

"Maybe not," Kruger responded with a shrug. They crossed

40

Prince Edward Boulevard and turned up toward the Europa. Tall, slender Bamileke women moved past them, swathed in orange, balancing baskets on their heads. Cattle wandered through the streets. The sun glared off the white fronts of the low buildings along the avenue. O'Reilley was already bathed in sweat when they reached the Europa and ducked in through the bead-curtained door.

"Eric! Paul! They let you out. I thought when they got hold of you they'd keep you." Madame Valéry rose from her stool and waddled toward them. An extremely heavy, dark-eyed woman who couldn't resist silk, she was a shrewd operator—she had to be to have become as rich as she was. The Europa was only one of her properties, but it was her pet. She spent most of her day in its cool confines, sipping rum punch as she worked at the bar, stacks of papers spread out before her and on the floor. She appeared older than she was, and was somewhat slovenly, perhaps even dull, but had a piece of everything that went on in the Cameroons, and some of it wasn't legal. O'Reilley didn't trust her enough to talk to her. Madame Valéry's single passion was and always would be the dollar. Or the franc. Or the mark.

"You boys owe me some money too," she said, sliding onto a chair to face Kruger and O'Reilley. "What a damn fool thing to do, starting a fight with Dupré. A person would think you wanted to go to jail." She turned her head and barked, "André! Rum punch three times."

"Two without the punch," O'Reilley said.

"You'll have no stomach by the time you're forty, Eric," said Madame Valéry, taking one of O'Reilley's hands between her own. Fingers like white sausages tapped against his palm. Her eyes roamed O'Reilley's face, taking in the coppery tan, the bristly hair that was nearly the same color, the pale eyebrows and dark green eyes, the once-broken nose, the thoughtful mouth and cleft chin. But she could make out nothing of his face. O'Reilley was a private man, Kruger too. Two more stranded people.

André, muttering to himself, brought the punch and the two

straight rums. When he was gone, Madame Valéry asked, "You boys have enough money? I can't see what you're living on."

"We have enough," O'Reilley yawned. "That last big load of ivory is still carrying us."

"Really? Seems to me that roll must be getting thin no matter how fat it was."

"You worry over us like a mother," O'Reilley said.

Madame Valéry laughed, and there might have been an edge of embarrassment to it. "Think I'm that old, eh? Well, maybe I could have had boys like you, too. So what's wrong with that?"

"Nothing, Madame Valéry."

"Maybe I just lust for you two big white hunters, eh?"

"Wouldn't doubt that either," O'Reilley said dryly, and Madame Valéry cut loose with a booming laugh.

"Okay. Well, I've offered help. I've got a couple of jobs open in the north."

"The gas fields?" Kruger asked, downing his rum.

"That's right. That gas is coming in, boys. If I could only get the damned equipment I need, I'd make a fortune."

"If they let you keep the gas."

"Who?" she flared up.

"The Third Reich, who else?"

"Screw the Third Reich. What does Captain Hofacker know anyway? He was in here last night with six or seven of his men. Dead drunk. He'll be a war casualty. His heart is going to go or his liver explode, I don't know which," she said, downing her punch and calling to André for another.

"How's the war going anyway?" she asked, leaing forward.

"Who the hell knows," Kruger said.

"I thought you two knew everything."

"Maybe Diels knows. Up until last month he had contact with Europe, but he's not going to tell us no matter which way it's going."

"It used to be exciting, you know that?" Madame Valéry said with a sigh. She leaned back, hanging a heavy arm over the back of her chair. "The war, that is. It was so far away, it

42

was kind of thrilling. How the hell did it ever get here? How the hell did we ever get on the side of the Germans?"

By "we," she meant the French. O'Reilley told her, "There's still a Free French army." Not that they were doing much the last time any of them had heard.

"I'd like to find out who blew up the airstrip, is what I'd like to do," the cabaret keeper said. "We used to get those guys in from Libya, those German pilots. They'd talk a little after they'd had a few drinks. Used to tell me all about what was going on." She tossed off her drink neatly and sighed again. "Now . . . who knows. I wouldn't be surprised to see the Führer show up—filthy pig—or a bunch of American marines."

"Not likely to see either," Kruger said.

"No." She looked beyond them, and her mouth tightened briefly before relaxing into a loose smile. "Hell, nothing ever happens in the Cameroons, does it?"

"It never will," O'Reilley said. His attention was no longer on Madame Valéry, however. The door behind the long bar had opened, the door that led to the sleeping quarters of the employees of the Europa. Michelle stood there, yawning appealingly. She wore a pale blue wrap, her dark hair flowing down across her shoulders. Her eyes met O'Reilley's and her jaw froze in midyawn. She smiled sheepishly and crooked a finger at him.

"What in the world's the matter with you?" Madame Valéry asked. She looked across her shoulder and complained, "Beaten by a younger *fille* again. What's the matter with you men, don't any of you appreciate experience? Well, I've still got you, Paul." She patted Kruger's hand.

"Sorry, Paul's going along with me," O'Reilley said, rising.

"Yes? Madmen. Now what is there for me to do but work?" She looked around the empty cabaret as if for prospects, then heaved her massive bulk upright. She rubbed Eric's head. "You—you stay out of troubles. And no more fights in my place . . . which is to remind you you owe me seven hundred and twenty francs for the damage."

"You'll get it," O'Reilley said. "I promise."

43

"When we have it," Kruger added.

"Yes—money for rum, no money for bills. Typical. Did I tell you about my second husband, Henri?" They were already walking away. Madame Valéry smiled knowingly, then turned back toward the bar, where André was polishing the glasses, still talking to himself as always. "Rum punch!"

O'Reilley had his hat in his hand as he rounded the end of the mahogany bar and wrapped his arms around Michelle, who turned her mouth up to him expectantly. Her lips were supple and warm. Their kiss lingered as Eric's hand roamed her back. When he withdrew, she was still looking up at him, her eyes wide and moist, her lips still parted.

"Business?" she asked.

"Business."

"Ah, well, then damn you, O'Reilley," she said, but she smiled as she said it. "Come on. How are you, Pauli?"

"I'm all right. Anyone been around?"

"No."

They followed her down the narrow hallway and into her room. After they had entered, Michelle locked the door and leaned against it, watching them with idle curiosity as they moved the table and tattered blue sofa and began prying up the floorboards.

"How are you going to get those out?" she asked.

"The window. Koko will be around with a cart."

"When? How do they know what to do?"

"It's all set up. Someone will have been watching the prison. They know we're out now."

"They'll know whites were involved," Michelle said. "You realize that, O'Reilley."

"Yes, darling."

"I don't like that tone, O'Reilley."

"No, darling."

The floorboards were coming up now, and Michelle checked the lock on the door again as Paul and O'Reilley began lifting the M-1s out of concealment. She trembled as she watched them, stacking the rifles to one side, the steel ammunition boxes to the other.

Sometimes she wondered why she had let herself get involved in something like this. Captain Hofacker might be a bloated alcoholic fool, but he was smart enough to take them off and hang them if the Germans got word of this. Getting discovered didn't seem all that unlikely either. There were scores of people in Douala who would turn them in in a minute for a few hundred reichsmarks. Times were tough.

Michelle looked at her man, still not understanding why she had volunteered her room for this.

There was a sudden, sharp knocking at the door, and Michelle felt the blood drain out of her, her legs grow weak. O'Reilley spun around, remaining in a crouch, his teeth bared, his body rigid, catlike.

"Yes?" Michelle said with a tremor in her voice.

"It's me, honey," Madame Valéry called. "Let me in."

"Uh . . ." Michelle's eyes darted to O'Reilley and back again. "I can't just now. A private conversation, you know."

"With both of them?" Madame Valéry laughed. "Come on, Michelle. There's trouble with the costumes. Let me in."

"I'll come out. In a minute."

There was a long wary pause before Madame Valéry replied in a stiffer tone, "All right, Michelle. Later." They heard her heavy footsteps recede, and Michelle spun angrily toward the two men.

"All right. Now you've done it. She's mad at me. Where else am I going to get a job in Douala if I get fired!"

"She's not going to fire you," O'Reilley said, hoisting another box of ammunition up from the cubbyhole. "She'll cool off fast; she always does."

"Yes? You know her better than me, huh, O'Reilley?" Michelle asked hotly. "I tell you, there's steel in that woman. And don't think she cares what happens to you."

"Calm down."

"Sure. Calm down. I must be crazy!" She ran a hand through

her dark hair, pushing it back from her forehead. "Always it's a man who makes trouble for me. I must be insane. Get those things out of here. Now! Nail the floor back down good. Next time it might be the Germans who knock." She walked to a corner chair and sagged there, her arms dangling between her outstretched legs. "Who cares anyway, O'Reilley? Who really gives a God damn if the Germans run this country or the English? Everything is the same as always. I just want the war to be over—you, you want to bring it to our doorsteps."

O'Reilley rose. "Watch for Koko, will you, Paul?"

Kruger glanced at Michelle, who still sat, head down, in the corner. "Sure."

O'Reilley walked over to her, tilting her reluctant chin up with his hand. "I'm sorry, Michelle. Look, we'll be gone in half an hour. I won't ever ask you to do anything like this again. We just didn't have much choice."

"Oh, hell," she said, biting her lip, turning her soft eyes on him. "You've got a hell of a memory. I volunteered, remember? I'm just not so tough, O'Reilley. You'd think I would be by now, but I'm not. Just get out, okay."

"Okay." He bent his head and kissed her, tasting the salt of a tear. The French girl laughed, hiccuped, and pushed him gently away.

"None of that, you'll have me in your army."

"Tonight?" he whispered against her round pink ear.

"Yes, you lousy bastard. Tonight." She started to stretch out her arms, then pulled them back, shaking her head. "Out! You too, Pauli, hear me?"

"Yes, darling," Paul said with a grin. She didn't have anything at hand to throw at the South African, and so she simply folded her arms sulkily, her breasts swelling against the silky slip she wore beneath the wrap. She sat again, ankles crossed, pouting as only a French girl can pout.

Paul was peering out the shuttered window when O'Reilley came up and laid a hand on his shoulder. "Not yet?" he asked.

"Nothing. Hope they didn't pick him up."

"What for?"

46

"Since when do they need a reason? He's Mesotho's nephew, isn't he?"

"He'll be along."

"I hope so, Eric," Kruger said. "I can just see us explaining this pile of American rifles to Hofacker or Brieux."

"He'll be along," O'Reilley repeated, only this time it seemed more of a hope than a conviction. Together they watched the parched, dung-spattered alley behind the Europa as the African sun rose into a fragile white sky.

He sat on the terrace of his white house, looking at the bird-of-paradise flowers, the crimson *bolukus*, and watching the sea breeze shift the leaves of the old rubber tree. The heat was oppressive. It drained a man, pressing against heart and lungs, sapping one's ambition. Walther Diels had a brief, vivid memory of the cold winds blowing through the plane trees outside the house in Dresden, where he had been born. Later they had moved to Hamburg, where his father, an electrical engineer, had died. Only fifteen, Walther had become the family's sole source of support.

He had left school and worked as a hod carrier and brick layer's apprentice before finding work in the bakery of Herr Tanner, a gruff, red-faced man with sixteen children. When Tanner spoke, it was with a roar, but he had taught Walther Diels the business of making bread and flaky strudel. When the old man died, Diels had carried on, running the bakery until Tanner's two oldest sons informed him that he was no longer needed.

After that, Diels entered the army. It was 1921 and Germany was deep in depression. It was a way to survive. In five years he was a lieutenant, transferred to the signal corps and then to the Abwehr, army intelligence. From there he had progressed steadily to his current rank of colonel.

There had been time to marry and father a daughter and a son. The girl, Susi, had died very young of influenza. August had grown to become a fine young man, an accountant until 1939, when he, too, had joined the Abwehr.

How was he now? What was happening in Germany? There had been no more reports after the curt message informing Diels that the Abwehr was dissolved, that he was relieved of his commission and ordered to return to Berlin. This last was surely a joke. There was no way out of the Cameroons. The dispatch planes had stopped coming six months ago—even before the airfield had been destroyed, the interlocking iron planks that covered the boggy ground spirited away, the tower radio smashed by Allied sympathizers.

If there was no longer an Abwehr, what had happened to August? Undoubtedly he had been absorbed into another arm of the service, but Walther couldn't even be sure of that.

One sat and watched the wind in the trees and remember Dresden long, long ago.

"There is lunch," said Frau Diels, and her husband turned slowly, looking up into her pinched, heavily lined face. She seemed to feel it was all his fault that he was no longer an Abwehr colonel, that they were stranded in this damnable African nation.

"Yes, thank you." He rose from the chair.

"It's not much. There isn't much, you know. Our savings are nearly gone."

"Yes. I'm not so hungry anyway. This heat . . ." He waved an arm aimlessly toward the crystal sky.

"I'm going into market. Though I don't know what I can afford. We'll soon be grubbing after insects like the natives."

Walther Diels didn't answer. There was no point in it. She was already tying on her straw hat, tucking her gray-streaked dark hair under it as he came into the house to seat himself in a cane chair before the table. His wife walked past him, tight-lipped, and went out, banging the door.

Diels poked at the bland dinner of boiled chicken and plantains, and drank a little wine. Heartburn rose in his chest. He pushed the wine away and went into the office, closing and locking the door behind him.

The house had once belonged to a French chargé d'affaires, and this had been his den. A glass-eyed leopard head still hung on the wall. The furniture in this windowless room was heavy and dark. Directly before Diels hung a scarlet-and-black emblem. A swastika—or, as the natives called it, the Iron Web. The cross enclosed in a circle was everywhere, and had been since the Germans had arrived. It resembled the local symbol for a spider's web.

It *was* a web, one that held Germany and a dozen other countries helpless while Hitler crept over them. Hitler and his new order, his new Germany, his secret police, his fanatical followers.

Diels turned sharply away from the symbol of all of that and walked to the highboy that stood in the corner. Touching the hidden latch, he lowered the false front. The secret radio had sat unused for months. There had never been anything to report, even when the lines of communication were open. Now Diels no longer tried.

Behind the radio was the folder. He hadn't known what to do with it. He withdrew it and thumbed through the papers it contained. *Dachau, Ravensbrück, Auschwitz, Sachsenhausen.* . . . Diels felt his stomach knot, and the bile begin to rise as it always did when he thought about what the New Order had accomplished.

And there was the primary document, the pointing finger. The order with *his* signature on it. The mind behind the New Order, the beast behind the savagery. Scrawled, the signature on the paper demanding the death of the millions was quite legible.

A. Hitler.

Diels looked aimlessly around the room, searching for a hiding place—somewhere the documents might be safe until after the war, when they could be given to someone, for Diels had decided long ago that he would not allow these criminals to get away with it. On that he and August had agreed the moment they had discovered the purpose of the "resettlement" camps so long ago, before Diels had come to the Cameroons.

Diels's chest had begun to burn again, and he rubbed it as he slowly paced the room. One day someone would come for the radio, he believed, and the papers must not be there when they did. His wife knew nothing of this, but if he were found out, she too would be killed. His main concern was not for his own safety, but for hers—and for that of the folder. *Where?*

In his desk drawer was a steel documents file. Diels emptied it of its contents and placed the folder containing the concentration-camp reports inside. He locked the box and opened the door to the office.

He called his wife's name, and when there was no answer, he went through the house, the box under his arm. Behind the building was an old whitewashed chicken coop. Diels opened the door and recoiled at the smell of decomposing manure.

Behind wire cages littered with feathers and droppings, a green snake slithered under the wall and out.

He found a weathered shovel and began to dig at the mountainous pile of manure beneath the cages. Finally, the box was beneath the manure, the pile raked over to appear untouched, and he went out again. He stood for a long moment looking toward the sea, blindingly blue through the palms.

Diels walked back to the house, wondering as his heartburn flared up and then gave way to a sharp, persistent pain what Frau Diels would manage to find to bring him for his supper.

5

Eric O'Reilley leaned back and flung the object he had carried from town over the cyclone fence. Then he pulled back into the shadows of the trees to crouch beside Paul Kruger and watch as the dog snuffled its way across the prison yard.

"Moon will be up in forty-five minutes," Kruger reminded O'Reilley, but the American gave no indication that he had heard.

The Alsatian found the joint, and growled with pleasure as it stripped the raw meat from the bone.

Kruger and O'Reilley stayed beneath the bamboo palm, watching. After a minute the dog lifted its head, shook as if its ears hurt, then backed slowly away from the meat. The Alsatian started to run, seemed to lose its balance, and circled back. Then it simply collapsed onto its side, flanks heaving for a few moments before it lay still.

O'Reilley rose, picking up the M-1 carbine beside him, and they moved to the fence. Paul had the wire cutters out and snipped open a three-foot flap while O'Reilley scanned the dark form of the prison, the M-1 cool in his hands.

Kruger nodded, flung the cutters away, and, Smith & Wesson .38 in hand, led the way through. They darted across the prison yard toward the kitchen. There were a few lights on inside—upstairs, where the offices were, and father along where the laundrymen worked late.

O'Reilley reached the wall, pressing his back to the stones, waiting for Kruger. Tossing his rifle to the South African, he got to work on the window lattice. The ancient strap iron came away easily as O'Reilley's gloved hands worked his tin snips.

After he had peeled back the bands of iron, O'Reilley gripped the ledge and hoisted himself up and into the deserted kitchen. They had exactly one hour before the cook and his helpers reported for duty. That was one of the many things they had learned from their night in jail.

The kitchen door was unlocked, as it had been earlier. O'Reilley swung it silently open. He chanced a quick glance into the lantern-lit corridor and saw the lone guard pacing the stone floor before Mesotho's cell.

If the legionnaire saw them he would have to be killed, or the game was up. O'Reilley's lips tightened as he again handed Paul his rifle, slipped the razor-edged bayonet from its sheath, and moved out.

The guard was facing in the other direction. In three paces, if he adhered to his pattern, he would turn back to face O'Reilley. If that happened, the bayonet would find his throat. The Frenchman's methodical habits saved him. He had taken only two steps when O'Reilley, on cat feet, reached him. O'Reilley's bunched fist and the haft of the knife slammed into the legionnaire's neck just below his ear. With O'Reilley's free hand around his mouth to stifle any groan, the Frenchman fell silently to the floor.

O'Reilley quickly checked the guard's belt, even though he knew he was not supposed to have cell keys. He didn't.

Glancing back, he moved ahead to the heavy oak-and-iron door across the corridor, the door that separated the petty criminals' block from that of the felons. Observation had revealed that a second guard sat there, and that the keys hung from an iron peg in the stone wall.

The corridor was silent. Flickering, smoky shadows cast by the lanterns painted dancing images against the walls.

O'Reilley reached the door and peered cautiously through the grill. Luck was with him; the guard's chair was unoccupied. And the keys hung in their accustomed place.

O'Reilley eased through the door, eyes darting toward the bend in the corridor where the guard might appear at any time. He hooked the key ring and stole back through the door, shutting it silently. Then, taking long strides, he returned to Mesotho's cell. He tried one key after the other, his fingers fumbling, his eyes shuttling constantly to the far door. He could hear the rustle of movement inside the cell, and as he finally found the right key and tripped the lock, he found Mesotho waiting, his fists bunched, his eyes yellow in the lantern light, his glistening black body coiled for an attack that never came.

"O'Reilley," he said almost breathlessly. His savagely, deliberately scarred face was obsidian in the darkness. His massive chest heaved with adrenaline.

"Come on. Quickly."

Mesotho hesitated for only a fragment of a second, then came forward, peering out into the corridor, where O'Reilley was already jogging back toward the kitchen.

Mesotho reached the doorway about the time O'Reilley did, impelled by the need to be free of this terrible place. "All's quiet," Kruger whispered, and together the three men went through the outer door, pausing in the shadows to let their eyes sweep the compound.

Then they moved, running in a low crouch until they reached the flap cut in the cyclone fence. They passed through, running among the bamboo palms and mahogany trees for a quarter of a mile before reaching the road. They stood still, panting for breath.

"Now, Mesotho?" O'Reilley finally asked. The moon was rising at O'Reilley's back, casting shadows on the ground and gilding the sea beyond the trees.

"Yes, O'Reilley. Now. You will show us how to shoot, and then we will rid this place of the Iron Web."

At the sound of a motor, all three men turned hastily. A legion truck was jouncing up the road, its headlights flickering.

"I am with you," Mesotho said again. "Now, however, I must leave you." With that, Mesotho took to the jungle once more, running as silently as the night wind, merging with the shadows.

O'Reilley and Kruger hit the ground as the whining truck whipped past them, leaving the stink of exhaust in the air.

"I hope," Kruger said, "you know what you're doing. Mesotho is unstable, you can see that."

"Got any other armies waiting in the bush, Paul?"

"No, but I wish to God I did. Those bastards are liable to go off on a tear, slaughter everything and everyone white they see. Arming them might be a mistake, Eric."

"It might be," O'Reilley said, rising, dusting himself off. "But it's war. We've got to take what allies we can get."

"Maybe." Kruger stood looking after the truck. "Maybe everyone's right. Maybe we ought to just wait and let the war blow over."

"You believe that?"

Kruger laughed. "No. I'm just a black-hating bastard, that's all."

"Are you, Paul?"

"There's only one sort of man I hate, Eric, and you know it. It's those that bow down to that damned bent cross."

"Then let's do it to them, Paul." He rested a hand briefly on the South African's shoulder. "And let's use whatever it takes. Get back to the Europa, all right? Build up an alibi for us if you can."

"You're not coming?"

"No," O'Reilley answered. "I've got a stop to make. I want to find out what our other potential allies are going to do when we touch off this wildfire. Better get the hunting rifles out of the Europa, Paul. I don't know where you can stash them, but that's no good anymore. Unless Hofacker's a bigger fool than I think, he'll cotton on that it wasn't Africans who broke Mesotho out tonight."

Paul took the M-1 and the bayonet, and O'Reilley, carrying the 9mm. Beretta he was never without—though it was a hanging offense to be caught with it—angled off through the moonlit mahogany forest.

The governor's mansion was well lighted despite the scarcity of fuel for the generator. As O'Reilley climbed the six-foot-high block wall behind the house and made his way through the withering peach trees, he heard the playing of a piano.

Slow, careless songs tossed off negligently in Ellen Henshaw's haphazard style.

O'Reilley walked through the back door without knocking. He spied Niko and motioned to him. "Please tell the governor I'm here. I'll wait in his study."

The African servant nodded, paused uncertainly, then headed off to fetch his master.

O'Reilley made his way down a dark corridor toward Lord Gore's study, where he lowered himself into a high-backed leather chair and waited.

"O'Reilley." Sir Harold Gore's nasal voice gave nothing away. "No need to sit in the dark." He turned on the electric lights—two bronze-shielded, flame-shaped bulbs beside the massive stone fireplace.

"Anything going on in town?" O'Reilley asked.

"No." Gore's eyebrows arched and drew together. "Why would you ask? Cigar?"

O'Reilley shook his head. "We just released Mesotho."

"God! You mean it? Of course you do." Gore ran his fingers through his thinning silver hair and sat in a chair opposite O'Reilley's, trimming his cigar. "Well, had to be done, of course. Can't get a commitment of any sort from Major Brieux."

"That's what I came to find out. How long is Brieux going to straddle the fence? I've heard him complain often enough that he was an unwilling lackey of the Germans, that he was French, that the Third Reich was the enemy of his country—yet he doesn't do a damned thing about it. He just follows the Vichy line."

"He's frightened, O'Reilley, that's all," said Sir Harold, slowly turning the tip of his cigar over the match's flame. "In a way he'd be performing a traitorous act to turn on the Germans, wouldn't he?"

"He's frightened," O'Reilley repeated in a low, flat voice.

"Yes."

"Do you know how many men Hofacker has at his post? I do, exactly. Forty-one."

"Armed with automatic weapons, I should point out. They have grenades and mortars as well. It wouldn't be easy to dislodge them."

"I think it would be. It's the last thing Captain Hofacker is expecting. And even if he were expecting it, he hasn't got the mental capacity to fight us."

"Your army," Gore said dryly, "is well trained, of course."

"There's an element of risk."

"You do see how it is," Gore said, leaning forward, brushing a bit of cigar ash from his pressed gray trousers. "Things are going along fairly smoothly. No one is harshly treated, except perhaps some of Mesotho's people. If we failed, O'Reilley, every non-German would be rounded up and probably killed. Certainly Brieux would be executed."

"Yes, I see how it is. I know how Brieux thinks. You, sir, how do you feel?"

"I? Well, it's war, isn't it, O'Reilley?"

"Yes, sir, it is."

"I'll talk to Brieux again. But I can't pretend to know what the man's response will be. It would make a difference, though, wouldn't it? Thirty-eight legionnaires on our side instead of the other."

"All the difference in the world, sir."

"You've given arms to the natives?" Gore asked, rising.

"Yes."

"Did you tell me where those rifles had come from? I've forgotten."

"We've had them under cover since 'forty-three. The Americans were considering sending in a commando group. Then General Gronowetter's battalion pulled out to reinforce Rommel in Libya, and I suppose the High Command decided the Cameroons simply weren't worth bothering about anymore. We've got the rifles, some ammunition, a case of black makeup they sent for local insurgents."

Gore smiled thinly. "What about you, O'Reilley? Your country doesn't feel the Cameroons is worth fighting for. Nor, apparently, does mine—maybe they're simply not able to spare the people. You—do you think it's worth dying for, this steaming, worthless land, now that the gold strikes have proven nearly worthless?"

"It's worth it," O'Reilley answered. "You said a minute ago that no one was really being bothered, except a few of Mesotho's people. Well, I've seen some of them after that mistreatment, sir. I've seen them used as slave labor—pregnant women, children, old men. They will be at it in the morning, in those gold mines. Some of them die every day. That's what's built up Mesotho's rage. When the war started, I really didn't give a damn. I haven't seen my own country in eleven years—besides, no one believes the Germans will ever get to the States. Just another war between the French, the Germans, and the British. One of those endless conflicts you people seem to dote on.

"I had no side. I'm in the Cameroons because Paul and I are stranded like the rest of you. It took me a while to see what was happening. Now I've seen it, sir. And yes, it's worth dying to stop it."

The door sprang open suddenly, and Ellen Henshaw stood there, studying them with her faintly mocking smile, her cool blue eyes shining in the soft glow cast by the lights beside the fireplace.

"I wondered what was up," she said.

"Sorry, my dear," Gore said smoothly. "Had a moment's business with Mr. O'Reilley."

"Quite all right, m'lord. I only wondered where you had gotten off to. Father was looking for you."

Father was Dr. Abel Henshaw, who, along with his daughter, had spent five years in this part of Africa. He had come from England to treat the terrible diseases that flourished in such tropical areas—or at least to try, depending on the inclination of the local witch doctors.

"Was it anything urgent, Ellen?"

"Just something he's discovered with the *Bacillus proteus*. He thought you'd be interested." Ellen looked at O'Reilley as she spoke, head up, her auburn hair piled high.

"I'll get along then," said Sir Harold. "I'll try to get back to you on that matter, O'Reilley."

"Right."

Gore glanced at Ellen, cleared his throat, and then went out. Still the woman remained. "What is going on, O'Reilley?" she asked finally in a furry voice that sent chills up the American's neck.

"In the outside world?"

"In *this* world. Lord Gore doesn't commonly meet people like you in his study, not at this time of the night, not behind closed doors. How did you get into the house, anyway?"

"I came in the back." O'Reilley moved nearer to Ellen, and her nose crinkled slightly. Eric still had on his dirty camouflage pants and a dark shirt. He towered over her, but the woman was obviously unintimidated. She simply tilted her head back and continued to gaze placidly into his eyes.

"May I ask why?"

"Why I came? Just a little private business. Nothing special or interesting."

"No." She paused, and Eric saw her mouth tighten slightly. A finely molded mouth it was, too, he thought, his eyes caressing the curved lines of her lips.

"I suppose it was nothing of interest to me. I only wondered . . . but then I suppose if I were to have to meet with Eric O'Reilley, I would do so as inconspicuously as possible."

"Really?" O'Reilley knew Ellen didn't like him, but he wasn't sure why. He had spoken with her from time to time since a clash between French and British forces in the interior had forced Ellen and her father to take shelter with Gore, but she had never warmed to him. The old charm just wasn't working.

Well, why would it? She knew he was undereducated, underbred, lacked visible means of support, and had declined to participate in the war. She undoubtedly knew about his living arrangements with Michelle in the cabaret. To top it all off, she was violently opposed to O'Reilley's profession, the slaughter of big game, a way of life which other women had found romantic, but which Ellen Henshaw thought disgusting.

She said, "Good evening," and, smiling that mocking smile, turned and started to leave the room. O'Reilley had a strong, sudden urge to reach out and grab her arm, to turn her and tell her—what? The impulse was quickly gone. And so, he observed, was Miss Ellen Henshaw.

He walked the empty streets back toward the Europa at a blistering pace, filling his lungs with the sea air, stepping into alleys when vehicles approached. Twice he saw the French police patrolling, once one of Captain Hofacker's roving patrols. From the back of their truck dangled a single black leg.

The Europa was as busy as it ever got when O'Reilley reached it. Kraus, whose family had been in the Cameroons since 1886, was there in a tropical suit, his greasy blond hair nearly falling into his drink as his head bowed reverently toward the rum.

In a far corner sat Roger Whiteshead, a British banker whose concern now had no assets to speak of, all specie and European currency having been confiscated for the Reich's use.

Sal Hurock, a fisherman, was there without his two hulking sons, and in the corner sat Madame Valéry with Paul and Michelle.

As O'Reilley sat beside Michelle, he felt the familiar pressure of her hand on his thigh. The owner of the Europa looked up.

"I suppose you've been here all night too," Madame Valéry said caustically.

"Of course," O'Reilley said with mock astonishment. Madame Valéry laughed, shaking her head. She reached out and patted O'Reilley's hand.

"You boys will end up being dragged through the streets, you know." She rose heavily, staggering under the influence of a full day's dose of rum punch. "I would change if I were you, O'Reilley. What is that blood on your sleeve?"

There was none, but O'Reilley's sharp glance downward told Madame Valéry all she wanted to know. She roared a laugh again. "It's a good thing I am not a gendarme, eh?"

A very good thing, O'Reilley thought as Madame Valéry moved away, her massive hips tilting and bulging beneath her green silk skirt. She called out a greeting to Kraus, whose head came up so sharply that he nearly fell off his barstool perch.

O'Reilley got up as well.

"Where are you going?" Michelle asked, her eyes wide and lustrous.

"To change."

"The door's locked. I'll have to let you in."

"Did you move our things, Paul?" he asked Kruger.

"Yes. I'll tell you about it later." He looked very sleepy—either the aftereffect of their earlier excitement, or from too many drinks.

O'Reilley left Paul to his drinking and followed Michelle up the hallway. When he reached the door, he tried the knob. The door swung open. "I thought you said it was locked."

"Did I?" She slipped past him, her eyes bright, and before O'Reilley had gotten the door locked from the inside she was out of her dress, standing in stockings and shoes for his approval. He approved.

Kruger was still drinking when O'Reilley returned. "I'd go light on that stuff, Paul."

"You would, would you? Why?"

"Tomorrow's going to be a busy day," O'Reilley said, looking around the smoke-filled cabaret.

"How busy, for instance?" Kruger asked cautiously.

"It's time, Paul."

Kruger was silent for a long minute. Then he nodded. "Okay. What about Brieux?"

"We can't wait for him forever. The hell with the French. We can only hope they'll stay out of the way."

"Tomorrow then."

"Tomorrow. Be here by five, will you? We want to get out to the Bamileke village before sunrise."

"Five o'clock huh? Hell of a time to start a war."

6

ERIC O'REILLEY CAME up slowly out of a heavy sleep. The room was dark. He felt the weight of Michelle against him, her smooth thigh thrown up across his legs, the mound of her breast against his arm, her tangled, profuse hair across his face and chest, the gentle stranglehold of her strong, slender arm. He lay there half-asleep, his mind slowly gathering itself. He was Eric O'Reilley. He was in a dark room in the Cameroons, Africa. And somebody was pounding the hell out of the door to Michelle's room.

He bolted upright, his temples throbbing. Michelle moaned. O'Reilley's hand slid beneath his pillow and grasped the cool butt of his Beretta automatic. It had to be the police or Hofacker's soldiers. They had been blown, damn it!

He moved to the door, holding the pistol beside his naked leg.

"Who is it?"

"It's me, Eric. Let me in, damn it!" Kruger's voice was low, excited, dry.

O'Reilley slid the latch and stepped back. Paul burst in, wearing a jacket over his pajama shirt, hastily tied deck shoes, and his khaki pants.

"What the hell happened, Paul? Did they come for you at the hotel?"

"No, nothing like that." Kruger sat down in a chair, paying no attention at all to Michelle, who sat up in bed, rubbing her head, the blanket falling away from her breasts.

"Then what?"

"Get dressed quickly. I'll show you. One of Koko's boys came and roused me."

"What *is* it, Paul?"

"Dress. You won't believe me. And bring your field glasses."

O'Reilley, still puzzled, was already dressing. Kruger sat drumming his fingers on his knees.

"Sorry I haven't any breakfast to offer you, Paul," Michelle said with heavy sarcasm. Kruger only grunted. Throwing the blanket around her shoulders and holding it together at her breasts, Michelle crossed the room and went padding down the hall toward the lavatory, muttering French oaths.

O'Reilley finished buttoning his shirt with one hand while he dug his Zeiss binoculars from his trunk. Kruger was already at the door, and with a nod of his head he went out, O'Reilley on his heels.

They cut through the storeroom and went out the back door of the Europa. Crossing Madame Valéry's scraggly garden, they stealthily angled through the stand of oil palms that lined the bay.

Kruger went to his belly and motioned O'Reilley to follow. Eric wriggled up beside his friend. The sun was not yet up, but there was just enough predawn gray to illuminate the water beyond the trees, and Eric saw it too. He began to slowly, methodically curse his luck.

He held the glasses on the submarine that was proceeding slowly across Victoria Bay toward the wharfs, looking for a berth. O'Reilley felt the pulse lifting in his throat. The swastika painted on the submarine's conning tower caught his eye, and he stared at it for a long while as the vessel advanced, nudging a thin white wake past its hull.

"Damn it all to hell," Eric said out loud.

Kruger had remained silent, as if he could be heard at that distance by the submarine. "See that deck gun?"

"I see it. Three point five, I think."

"They could cover all of the town with that. This time of year that submarine could navigate the Sanaga as far as Mesotho's village, if the sub commander has the nerve."

"How many in a submarine crew, Paul?"

"I don't know. Thirty, forty?"

"It just about doubles the German force in Douala."
O'Reilley watched as the sub eased up the deserted quay. "What
in hell could they want here?"

"No telling. But we've got to delay things until they're gone,
Eric."

"Yes." He lowered the glasses and handed them to Kruger.
"Get word to Mesotho, will you."

"He's liable to try it anyway. He wasn't too happy when he
came out of prison."

"If he does, he's leading his people to their deaths."

Kruger left to send a runner out to Mesotho's camp to tell
the Bamileke chief that there was trouble; to hide the M-1s
and keep low. But Mesotho was liable to ignore these orders.

When the South African returned, the sun was up, the eastern horizon red and angry. O'Reilley still lay in the palms, still
watched the docks.

"What's up?"

"Here they come. Now we'll find out something."

O'Reilley shifted his elbows and steadied the glasses. The
first man out was a sailor in naval whites. Three or four others
followed, and they began securing the submarine, placing a
plank, doing something O'Reilley couldn't make out aft.

"Take it for a while, Paul," O'Reilley said, handing the Zeiss
glasses to Kruger. An hour dragged past. The day was already
hot. Sweat rolled off of both men. The sea became a glittering,
tessellated mirror. A baboon moving through the trees stopped
when it saw the hunters, went to its hind legs and bared three-
inch fangs, then continued on its way, glancing cautiously back.
Nearby a Sharpes's parrot shrieked.

"They're forming up now," Kruger said, and O'Reilley rolled
over, eyes alert. "Uh-oh," Paul muttered.

"What is it?"

"You won't like this. *Schutzstaffel*, and they've got automatic
weapons—can't make out the type. Here." He returned the
glasses to O'Reilley, who grimaced with disgust.

SS men, and, as Paul had said, they carried submachine guns.
They now stood on the dock in their gray uniforms. Their

leader, who looked to be a standartenführer, a full colonel, wore parade black, the silver death's head on his cap. He, however, was SD.

Now O'Reilley picked up movement to his left, and he switched the glasses to where a naval officer in whites was walking forward, a tall, fair man with a hitch in his gait. He was followed by a sailor built like a block of granite, and another, darker officer.

"SS," Kruger said under his breath. "What for, O'Reilley? Surely not for us. Then what? What in the hell do the bastards have in mind for Douala?"

O'Reilley let his field glasses settle on the face of the SD colonel. Bulky, heavily jowled, red-cheeked, with a small, hooked nose. His expression—or what O'Reilley could see of it—was purposeful but dispassionate: a bad combination. Eric didn't speculate on what was coming; he didn't think he wanted to know.

Walther Diels awoke in a sweat. His ears were ringing, his throat was dry. He lay in his tangled bedding, staring at the ceiling. He glanced at the other bed, but Frau Diels was up and gone.

Diels had gotten into the habit of sleeping late. There was no longer any reason to rise. There was no more 5:00 A.M. Tokanga-relay message. There was, he thought, no Tokanga relay. There was no Abwehr, and on mornings like these it seemed there was no war. There were no shots, no marching soldiers, no bombs falling. Only the oppressive heat, the shrieking of parrots, the muffled hiss of the wind in the trees, the occasional distant roar of an excited mandrill, the cold eyes of his wife. He rolled over and tried to go back to sleep, but he found he could not lie on that side. His arm hurt. It would hurt and then go numb. Ever since he'd finished the shoveling the day before, he'd felt sick. For a man unused to exercise, a man of Diels's age, the activity had not been good. He felt the fire in his chest and cursed the heartburn that never seemed to go away. He awoke with it, he went to bed with it.

When Diels started to sit up, he found with amusement and concern that his left leg would not respond to his brain's commands.

"It's still asleep," he said to himself.

Massaging his leg, he managed to restore a semblance of feeling, but when he swung it toward the side of the bed a sharp pain shot through his entire left side. It subsided, leaving him with a strange light, slightly dizzy sensation.

"That's odd," Diels told the empty room. Now, with feet firmly on the floor, he tried to rise. Pain arced through his body from his toes to his skull. His left arm seemed to be on fire and there was a sudden, sharp seizing in his chest as if a great hand had thrust itself through his ribs and clamped down on his heart. He felt bile rising in his throat and nostrils, felt his knees buckle, felt his face slam against the floorboards. Then he felt nothing. He was awake, alert, but he felt nothing. Nor could he move. He simply lay there, his eyes pleading, his heart racing as he opened his mouth and attempted a scream that would not come.

"How long ago did this come in?" Captain Konstantin Hofacker shouted at his aide. In his hand was a radiogram, which he waved excitedly. Hofacker's aide looked at his superior, who was dressed in uniform trousers and pajama top. His eyes were red, his face pale, eyes hollow. The few strands of dark hair he possessed, which were usually carefully placed across his yellowish scalp, now hung into his eyes and across his ears.

"The message was given to me at oh-three-thirty, sir," the lieutenant said.

"Then why in the hell did you wait until now!"

"I was under your strict order, sir," the lieutenant reminded the commander of the Douala garrison. "You were with a young woman, and you ordered me not to disturb you—even if the Führer himself wished to see you."

The lieutenant kept a straight face, but amusement danced behind his eyes as Hofacker, still groaning, tried to dig his boots out from under the bed. The captain's forehead wrinkled with each pulse. He was wearing a nasty hangover.

"See that the staff car's readied immediately," Hofacker said from the floor, "and see that she"—he motioned with his head toward the bathroom door—"is off the post within ten minutes."

"Yes, sir." The lieutenant didn't have to wait for "her." The bathroom door opened, and an African girl of eighteen or so with a solid, lithe body which possessed—as Hofacker could have confirmed—astonishing strength, emerged.

"Out!" Hofacker shouted. "Give her something, Lieutenant. Tinned beef, sugar, anything handy, and get her out!"

"Yes, sir," his aide answered, still suppressing the smile. He inclined his head, and the naked African girl followed him out the door as Hofacker cursed and groaned alternately.

An SD colonel was arriving—had already arrived—and here he was undressed, unshaven, alcoholic tremors running through him.

What in God's name was the SD doing here? With a party of Schutzstaffel. In the Cameroons, for Christ's sake! Hofacker was perspiring as he finally found his missing boot and sat on the bed to pull it on. He was always perspiring in this damnable, disease-ridden country. He lived on whisky and quinine tablets.

"The car's warming up, sir," Lieutenant Neurath said, poking his head in the door. "Did you wish me to accompany you?"

"Is the girl gone?"

"Yes, sir. I gave her a bolt of cloth and a sack of sugar."

"It wouldn't look too good, you see. The SD man must not know, Neurath. A black one! God, they'd have me in a KZ."

"It is," the young lieutenant said suavely, "our secret." Satisfied that he now had a hold on his commanding officer, Lieutenant Neurath was entirely amiable.

"Wait in the car for me, Neurath. I'll have to shave."

When the captain emerged from the headquarters building, his face was bleeding slightly in three different places. He climbed into the backseat of an open Mercedes 500K that had two pennants attached to the front bumper, the insignia of the Third Reich, the bent iron cross, and Hofacker's own insignia which only yesterday had seemed dashing, but now appeared pretentious.

Neurath was sitting in the car, impeccably dressed, clean-shaven. He was not smiling, not at all, but one had the *impression* he was smiling. The driver slapped the car into gear, and the Mercedes rolled out through the gate and onto the arrow-straight dirt road that led through the palms toward the city.

The jungle thinned and then parted, and Douala, yellow-bright in the morning sun, hove into view. The streets were busy with bicycle traffic, peddlers, and market-bound shoppers. Beyond glittered the sea. The Mercedes, still moving at great speed, hit Prince Edward Boulevard and wheeled toward the docks.

They were waiting when Hofacker arrived, and it appeared as if they had been waiting for some time. SS men sat or stood in the shade cast by the disused African Oil barn. A few sailors moved about on the submarine, one of them with an oilcan in hand.

The Mercedes braked to a hard stop, and Hofacker saw the SD colonel strolling toward him, face shaded by the bill of his cap, hands behind his back, holstered Luger riding against his thigh.

"Hofacker?"

"Yes, Herr Colonel. I was unavoidably detained."

"Where are the trucks?"

"Trucks, Herr Colonel?" Hofacker said nervously. He realized suddenly that he had neglected to salute, and now it was too late to amend the oversight. His head hammered away, despite the six aspirin he had gulped down. He squinted into the sun off the sea. The colonel spoke again.

"I must somehow convey my people to your camp, Captain Hofacker. Trucks would seem the obvious method."

"Yes, Herr Colonel," Hofacker said, his throat tight and dry. "See to it, Herr Lieutenant," he snapped at Neurath, who snapped his arm up, shouted, "Yes, Commandant, Heil Hitler!" and departed at a jog trot. It was then that Hofacker decided he hated his aide.

"Please take me to the house of Walther Diels," Colonel Olbricht said. He was sweltering in his uniform. It must have been a hundred and ten degrees.

"Yes, Herr Colonel, immediately." Hofacker held the door open, and the colonel, after signaling two of the SS men to join him, stepped in.

Olbricht was flanked in the backseat by Erzberger and Ziegler. Hofacker had no choice but to climb into the front next to the driver. Hofacker gave his instructions sharply, and the corporal nodded, turning the car around and heading back uptown.

Hofacker draped an arm over the back of the seat and turned to ask, "Might I inquire what brings you to Africa, Herr Colonel Olbricht?"

"It shall all be explained later," Olbricht said. Hofacker noticed the rivulet of perspiration trickling from beneath the colonel's hatband, running down across his forehead.

"Yes." He turned around and made a point of directing the driver, who knew perfectly well where the Abwehr officer's house was.

When the open car pulled up in front of Diels's palm-screened house, there was already a lot of activity. Olbricht saw a black man who was carrying something run away from the house. The front door stood open. A woman appeared there briefly and then disappeared inside. Olbricht climbed out, his hand automatically touching the flap that covered his Luger.

"What is happening here, Hofacker?" Olbricht asked.

"I couldn't guess, sir."

No, Olbricht thought, you couldn't. In tandem, the two German officers moved across the brown lawn, the SS men behind them, automatic weapons in hand. Ziegler's eyes gleamed with anticipation.

Hofacker paused to rap on the doorframe, but Olbricht had already brushed past him and entered the house, boot heels ringing. Ziegler had snicked off the safety on his weapon. Olbricht, his mouth dry, drew his own sidearm without really knowing why.

There seemed to be a great deal of activity in the rear of the house. They could hear voices, soft and concerned.

Olbricht saw the woman leaning against the doorjamb and called out sharply, "Frau Diels!"

"Yes." She turned, her arms folded, her mouth tight, appearing annoyed.

"I am Colonel Olbricht, SD. I must see your husband at once."

"Yes." The woman's eyes met those of Olbricht and then swiftly searched Hofacker and the two SS men. "He's in there."

Diels lay on the bed, his face bluish white. Over him was crouched a white-haired, spectacled man with soft hands and a competent manner.

"What is the meaning of this?" Michael Henshaw asked without turning. He glanced across his shoulder and repeated his question in German.

"Who are you? What is wrong with Herr Diels?"

"Herr Diels has had a stroke. I am Dr. Henshaw."

"Britisher?"

Henshaw didn't bother to answer the question. Olbricht heard the rustle of fabric behind him and he spun, starting to bring his Luger up before he realized that the newcomer was an elegant, quite beautiful woman. She carried a covered tray.

"Pardon me," Ellen Henshaw said, sparing one of her most contemptuous glances for the colonel. Then she walked to the bed where her father worked over Diels.

"Can he speak now? When will he be able to speak?" Olbricht asked. He had moved nearer to the bed, and now he saw Diels's eyes reach out and clutch at his own. His mouth moved soundlessly.

"He certainly cannot speak now," Henshaw said sharply. "He is in grave danger of losing his life. Please! You men will have to leave."

Olbricht stood there a minute longer, holstering his automatic, watching Diels struggle for life.

"Frau Diels! We must search your house."

"Yes, of course," she said, as if with secret amusement. Glancing back to the bed, her expression changed. She looked, Ellen thought, as if Diels had betrayed her by falling ill, had committed a disgusting, antisocial sin. Of course, Frau Diels had worn that expression constantly since her husband had been relieved of his duties when the Abwehr was dissolved.

"You will show us where your husband worked, please," Olbricht commanded. The German woman nodded and led the way out.

"Filthy—" Ellen began, but her father glanced at her and shook his head.

"Where in the world did they come from?" he asked. Ellen didn't answer. After another minute her father stood. "I can't do anything else. No one could."

"Will he survive?" she asked, knowing full well that with strokes one never knew.

"He may." Henshaw was wiping his hands, looking toward the doorway. "He may survive long enough to wish he hadn't."

They went out together, leaving a servant to watch Diels. One of the SS men had remained behind. He now stepped out before them, automatic rifle across his chest, and Ellen gave an involuntary gasp that seemed to please the man. He was huge, with close-cropped dark hair, a scarred chin, and eyes that flickered with an animal passion. He let those eyes sweep up and down Ellen now and she felt her stomach heave.

"Please follow me. The colonel wishes to see you," the man said.

The doctor shrugged, and they moved ahead of Ziegler, who strode imperiously behind them. They found Olbricht in Diels's office. The highboy had been torn open, exposing a radio Henshaw had never known about. They had rolled up the carpet and cut open the cushions of the settee. Now the other SS officer, a tall, blue-eyed man, was preparing to tear the paneling from the walls. The first strip came away with a loud crack.

"Ah, the doctor . . . what did you say your name was?"

"Henshaw."

70

"And your nurse?"

"My daughter, Ellen."

"I see. You are living with the Dielses?"

"No. We're next-door, in the governor's house."

"The governor?"

"The former governor, Lord Gore."

"The governor's house is that large white building beyond the trees?"

"Yes."

"Inform this Lord Gore that I shall be staying there. It will give us all an opportunity to get to know one another." And it was near to the Diels's house. "Frau Diels, you will see that food is provided for my personnel."

"Yes, Herr Colonel."

"And Doctor, you will inform me immediately if there is any change in Herr Diels's condition."

"Yes," said Henshaw. "I will."

"Then"—Olbricht rubbed his hands together—"that is all settled. There is nothing further to be done here at the present time, unfortunately. Suppose, Captain Hofacker, you show me your camp and the town itself. If I am to be held up in the Cameroons for a time, I should like to know something about it."

"Yes, sir," Hofacker said with relief. He felt himself out of the woods now. "It would give me great pleasure."

Leaving Erzberger and Ziegler posted at the house, the officers went out across the lawn. Olbricht noticed Ellen walking back to the governor's mansion with her father and allowed his eyes to enjoy her graceful, slim-hipped walk.

"Sir?" Hofacker was holding the door to the car open, and Olbricht grunted and stepped in.

"Slowly through the town, if you please," the army captain told the driver. The Mercedes rolled into motion, and Hofacker, leaning back in the seat, said, "You will find things quite different here, I would suppose."

They weren't different enough. As Hofacker completed his sentence, they heard the crack of a rifle and saw the driver's head explode. The Mercedes swerved violently as Olbricht tried to grab the wheel, hold on, and spot the attacker simultaneously. The car careened into a large teak tree, and Olbricht was thrown out of the backseat to slam into the shattered windshield. Hofacker was holding his face and moaning. Blood seeped through his fingers.

A second rifle shot caused Olbricht, his teeth bared, to leap from the car and press himself to the dusty street. Three more shots punched through the bodywork of the Mercedes before Olbricht spotted the black man with the rifle and emptied his Luger in that direction.

The African took to his heels, sprinting through the palms, holding his rifle by the barrel. He was heading behind the governor's house. He threw away his rifle and raced on toward the wadi beyond the peach grove.

He never made it. He emerged from the trees to find the uniformed man waiting, a machine gun at the ready. Ziegler triggered his weapon, and the bullets riddled the African's body, jerking him crazily before he tumbled back and lay sprawled against the grass. Then Ziegler stepped nearer and put a single round through the African's neck. The body shuddered at the impact and then lay still. Ziegler shouldered his submachine gun and started off at a trot to find his commander.

The war had come to Douala.

7

"WHAT IN THE hell was that?" Eric O'Reilley got up from his chair in the Europa and stared at Paul Kruger, who could only shrug in response.

"We'd better find out." Another series of shots rang out.

"Eric!" Michelle was clinging to him. "Don't go."

He shook the girl off, and he and Kruger went out into the blistering heat of midday Douala. Africans were rushing up the street toward the governor's mansion and Kruger started to run with them.

They had just reached the house when a truck rolled up the road and SS men began spilling out of the back. "You there!" an NCO called out, his weapon leveled, "What are you doing?"

A red-faced officer appeared from the other side of the truck and shouted in German, "What are you doing? Does this man look black to you, Corporal Wecke?" To O'Reilley he said, "Clear out of this area, please. There has been trouble."

O'Reilley merely nodded, then turned back down the path. When he looked back, the two soldiers were still watching him.

Kruger was half a block away. "It was Koko," the South African told him. "I got the story from someone who saw it. He laid an ambush for the Germans. Potted at them with the M-1, then took to his heels when the SD colonel returned his fire. He ran into a soldier with a submachine gun. There isn't much left to look at."

"God damn it," O'Reilley said with deep frustration. "Why?"

"Presumably because he was fused and ready to go. When we called it off because of the newcomers, Koko decided to do a little damage on his own."

"Yes, and what about Mesotho now? He's going to be out for blood. Next we'll have *him* assaulting a machine gun."

"We can talk to him," Kruger said hopefully.

"He won't listen to us now, Paul."

"He might. It's worth a try."

"Yes. We have to try, I suppose," O'Reilley said, removing his safari hat to run a hand across his damp copper-colored hair. "But not just now. God knows what Hofacker and his guest are conjecturing, but Mesotho is bound to cross Hofacker's mind."

They stepped out of the street as the approaching car rumbled up the dusty road.

"Brieux," Paul said sourly.

It was the Vichy French commander. Six legionnaires stood on the running boards, clinging to the doors as the ancient Fiat rolled by. They could see Brieux looking unconcerned, nearly bored, his narrow face with its General de Gaulle nose pointed straight ahead.

"I'm glad I don't have to watch him bow and tug at his forelock," Kruger said with some bitterness. They were nearing the Europa again. Before they entered, Paul asked, "What do you think they'll do about this, Eric?"

"You know the Nazis." O'Reilley shrugged.

"Yes." Kruger turned that around in his mind. Koko's wild act could bring fiery rain down on his tribe.

"Yes," Major Pierre Brieux of the French Foreign Legion was saying as he straightened up from examining the dead African, "he's Bamileke. As a matter of fact I know this one. His name is Koko. He's the nephew of our local rebel."

"Rebel?" Olbricht stopped mopping his perspiring forehead and looked sharply at the Frenchman, whose German was execrable.

"Yes. Mesotho is the man's name. He's anti-white. Wants all the Europeans out of his country."

"You have him incarcerated, of course?"

"We, uh, had him incarcerated, sir. However, he escaped last night from Victoria Prison."

"Then he must be found. It seems clear he was behind this criminal act."

"Yes, sir." Brieux swatted at swarming gnats before his face. "Do you want me to handle this, or is it Hofacker's responsibility?"

"I do not care who does it, only do it!"

"Major Brieux speaks the native language, sir," Hofacker put in weakly.

"Ziegler!" Olbricht called loudly. "Collect our men. We're leaving."

Ziegler saluted with a raised, stiffened arm and started shouting commands to the SS men. "Together," Olbricht said, "we shall visit this Mesotho's village."

"I'm sure we won't find him there," Brieux said placidly. "He'll have taken to the bush."

"Then we will search."

"Most difficult," Brieux said. "Nearly hopeless, I would say." Olbricht looked at the Frenchman, whose eyes revealed nothing.

"I refuse to stand by and do nothing. That encourages further incidents. This man killed a German soldier."

"He has been punished," Brieux said, looking at the lifeless, twisted body. Flies crawled over Koko's unfeeling dark skin.

"I want this Mesotho," Olbricht said firmly. He turned and strode toward the legionnaire's car, Hofacker and Brieux behind him. Hofacker was nervous and edgy, obviously in need of a drink. Brieux was impassive.

Brieux gave orders to his driver and the car started forward; through the back window, Hofacker could see the truck behind them carrying SS men.

They followed the rutted red road into the uplands. Dense jungle lined the trail on either side, broken here and there to reveal bizarre, barren cinder cones. They emerged eventually on a wide dry-grass upland dotted with hills.

"What is that?" Olbricht asked. He was pointing toward the

cleared knoll, where long lines of Africans could be seen moving up and down, some carrying baskets. A handful of German soldiers stood nearby.

"The gold mine, sir. Those working are Bamileke. There's really not enough quality ore here to make the working of the mine profitable."

"The labor is free, Captain," Olbricht reminded him, and at the same time the SD colonel wondered what was becoming of the gold. It wasn't finding its way to Germany, not with things the way they were. It would bear looking into.

"Here we are. Just ahead there, sir," Brieux said. Olbricht peered into the sun and made out the mud-and-straw huts, saw the women and children sprinting for the jungle as the army vehicles rumbled in.

"They're afraid we need more labor for the mine," Hofacker said.

"Or afraid we know about their rebellion."

"It didn't have the earmarks of an organized attack," Brieux put in. "One man, a little crazy perhaps."

"Yes—if we could be sure of that," Olbricht said in a way that made it clear *he* wasn't.

The Fiat braked to a stop, dust rolling across the Bamileke camp. Olbricht was out quickly, his pistol in hand as he looked around the village. The SS men coming at a run, machine guns in hand, didn't even break stride as Olbricht commanded, "Search this village. Every hut. Bring all prisoners to me."

Brieux watched from beside the car, touching a handkerchief to his mouth as the SS men stormed across the village, approaching each hut as if it were a pillbox. The sun was appallingly hot. The humid air was heavy; each breath seemed to fill the lungs with steam.

At the end of an hour, the SS had captured only three Bamilekes—one old man and two children. The old man was taken aside by Olbricht, Brieux, and Hofacker. Ulrich Ziegler stood by patiently, like an attack dog waiting to be set free.

"Ask him where Mesotho is."

Brieux did so. There was no response.

"Tell him this assassin, Koko, is dead. Tell him that his entire tribe will be eliminated if there is another attack."

Brieux explained that more carefully. "It is true," he said. "These men will kill everyone. Women and children as well."

"I understand that," the white-haired old man answered. "Ask him this—why doesn't he go home?"

"What did he say?"

"He says he wishes to help you in any way possible, but no one has seen Mesotho since he escaped from jail. He must have gone to the far mountains to hide from the mighty German warriors."

Olbricht stood rocking on the balls of his feet, hands behind his back. "All right. Leave the old man to tell the tale. The two children are to go to the labor camp. The village—destroy it!"

Ziegler looked disappointed. There was no one to kill, but he was somewhat mollified by the impending destruction. They heard the truck roar to life, saw Ziegler on the running board, directing the driver as he aimed the front bumper of the vehicle at the huts, smashing the mud and straw houses to ruins, the great wheels crushing household articles, toys, weapons, every possession. Other huts had been torched, though they burned poorly, and black curtains of smoke rose above the teak and mahogany forest into the pale African sky.

It was not until every hut, every belonging of the village that had sheltered six hundred people, had been destroyed that Olbricht was satisfied. Then he told Brieux he had a parting word for the old man, who stood watching in puzzlement.

"This is nothing—tell him that, Brieux—this is because I assume that the attack on the German force was the individual act of a madman. If there is a second attack, it will not be mud huts which are crushed into the earth, but the bodies of his people. Tell him this as well—I offer one thousand deutsche marks for the head of the man called Mesotho."

Turning before Brieux had finished translating, Olbricht walked back to the Fiat and sat there sweltering as the smoke drifted across the village and the children cried.

"I suggest you strengthen your street patrols, Major Brieux."

"Yes, Colonel Olbricht." Brieux closed the door sharply. He sat expressionlessly watching the village until the driver started the car and turned it back toward Douala.

"I saw no German soldiers on the streets," Olbricht said on the road back. "I cannot understand such laxity, Captain Hofacker. No wonder there can be an assault on German officers in broad daylight. You will detach that part of your force not needed for watching the labor camp and institute patrols."

"Yes, sir."

"This will not happen again!" Olbricht looked toward the sea. "If it does, there will be no place remote enough for these savages to hide." He had another thought. "I will inform the ex-governor, this Lord Gore, that there will be a dinner party tonight at his mansion. All respectable Europeans will be invited. Let us get to know one another."

And, Brieux considered, give Olbricht a chance to look over the opposition. It must have occurred to Olbricht as it had to him that the African assailant had had a rifle. None had been reported stolen, however. So where had it come from? Africans were forbidden to possess firearms, yet Koko had had one.

Brieux was convinced that the jailbreak had been engineered by whites, and he was halfway convinced that he knew who the two white men were. Halfway. He leaned his head back and watched the trees flicker by, wondering if his white dress uniform would be appropriate for an evening party with the governor.

Rudi Johst ordered another rum, since that was all they seemed to have for sale in that clip joint, and turned on his barstool to watch as the lights dimmed and the pretty little French girl with the wide soft eyes and the low-cut, sequined dress stepped up onto the platform in the back of the Europa. Half-closing her eyes, she began to sing to the accompaniment of an accordion.

Johst couldn't follow the French lyrics, but the song, low and sultry, tugged at him. The girl's voice, if not magnificent, was competent, but it was the shadow of sadness across the simplicity of the tune that rang true—regardless of the words. Johst grinned to himself. Maybe it was just that he had been too long without a woman, and there seemed small chance of finding one in this hole.

The French girl—now there was a beauty, and a lively one, Johst would have bet, but her eyes were fixed on the man seated beside the stage. British, was he? Maybe American, and Johst knew there was no chance of getting close to her either. Rum was a good second choice, so he slapped Horst Best on the arm and said, "Two more, eh, Horst?"

Half of the U-191's crew was in the Europa, and now, as the liquor began to warm them, they grew voluble and the laughter flowed more easily. The locals were wary of them, understandably, but Johst saw two of his men talking to a civilian who looked to be German bourgeois. Stutters and Reinhardt had been joking with the massive Frenchwoman who seemed to own this place.

Johst found another drink before him, and he folded his huge forearms on the bar and stared at it for a while, listening to the mild applause that followed Michelle's number.

He hesitated over his drink. Neither the captain nor Lieutenant Fritzche had said so, but he supposed he was responsible for keeping the rest of the submariners out of trouble. Recklessness was to be expected after the long confinement.

He heard the cabaret hush and, glancing over his shoulder, saw the SS man strut in. It was that damned Ziegler, with two regular army men behind him. He walked slowly around the cabaret, examining everyone there. While he spoke to one, Johst picked up his glass, drained it, and belched loudly.

"Your name, please?" the big, scarred SS man was saying with a veneer of politeness.

"O'Reilley." Eric let his hand slowly drop toward his belt line. The Beretta was thrust behind his waistband, covered by his loose blue shirt.

"Yes. You and this one." He nodded at Paul, who tensed, shot a glance at O'Reilley, and waited with breath held.

"We're to follow you?" O'Reilley asked cautiously. This, he was thinking, was a strange arrest.

"Of course not. You are to be at the governor's mansion tonight. Nine o'clock; please dress." With that, Ziegler moved away, searching the other faces. O'Reilley sagged with relief. Paul Kruger laughed nervously.

"A party. How wonderful."

"It means they haven't caught Mesotho—or haven't gotten him to talk. Otherwise our invitation would have taken a different form."

"What's behind this, though?"

"The SD colonel, I imagine. Wants to have a look at the competition, count heads, see who's going to be trouble."

"And then?"

"*Then* comes the arrest," O'Reilley said, glancing at his watch. "I suppose we'd better be there or they'll wonder why."

"You, too!" Madame Valéry descended wrathfully upon them as they rose to move away from the table. "*You?* You're invited to the governor's house, but not me! You two are respectable? In a pig's eye!"

O'Reilley kissed her cheek as she tried to pull away. He grinned and said, "It's the old Irish charm."

By eight o'clock O'Reilley was ready, shaven, dressed as formally as possible. A suit was seldom called for in Douala.

Kruger rapped on his door and came in. "Ready?"

"As ready as I'm going to get. How do you like the suit?" O'Reilley ran his hands down across the breasts of his tan worsted jacket.

"Warm?"

"Not really."

Outside, the night was star-bright and muggy. The town seemed nearly deserted but for the long-horned, hump-shouldered cattle that wandered the streets—and the German patrols rattling past in motorcycles equipped with sidecars, or standing silently in the shadows of the alleys.

"Where'd that suit come from, Paul?"

"Katanga. Remember? Six months in the bush and then we baked in that sauna drinking whisky until we couldn't stand up. We sold the ivory to Bennett and decided to get some suits made by the Chinaman. That was the week we met those missionary women."

"I'd forgotten. God, how long ago was that, five years?"

"About."

They were nearly at the governor's house. They could see lights blazing away upstairs and down.

"You know, Paul, we could pull out. Back to the bush. We've got our rifles and ammunition. We could stay out back until this is all over. Maybe raft down to Mbandaka, then take a riverboat or head overland to Leopoldville. Things are supposed to be quiet there."

They had stopped in the shade of a wind-shifted palm. Kruger's answer was only a shrug. "If it sounds good to you."

"What do you think?"

"I think we're in this too deep to walk out. I don't think you're serious about turning your back on it. It's been a bad day, that's all." He slung an arm over O'Reilley's shoulders. "Let's see what kind of party Sir Harold can throw these days." He paused. "Unless you were serious. In that case, let's pick up our rifles and get out of here. Now."

"No. No, I wasn't serious. As you say, Pauli, it's just been a very bad day."

Ellen Henshaw sparkled, despite her obvious disdain for the goings-on. She stood at the door beside the governor, greeting the guests. Not having invited anyone, they were both surprised by some of the guests.

"What *is* this?" Ellen hissed after Sal Hurock and his two burly sons, all reeking of fish, had entered the hall. "What in the world did Olbricht invite these people for? Surely not for conversation. There's men here I'd cross the street to avoid meeting. Oh no," she uttered plaintively. Beyond the two SS guards who stood beside the walkway leading to the mansion, she saw more unwelcome faces.

"Did you think he wouldn't be here?" Lord Gore asked wryly.

"I suppose I was hoping." She watched the two approach.

"I rather like O'Reilley myself," Gore commented. "Can't say why, but I do."

Ellen was going to answer, but she fell silent as Kruger and O'Reilley mounted the steps. O'Reilley's eyes were on her face, then sweeping down her pale blue dress, taking in the curve of hip, the narrow waist, the firm shelf of her breasts. She stifled a cutting remark. This was going to be a night of suffering.

"Good evening," said Lord Gore. "Welcome, Mr. Kruger."

"Are they going to lock us all in and take us away?" Paul asked lightly. Lord Gore was taken aback for a moment. He managed a smile.

"Certainly hope not, old boy. And I wouldn't speak like that inside, were I you."

"Which dance is mine?" O'Reilley asked mischievously.

Ellen replied, "I am afraid we will have no music this evening, Mr. O'Reilley."

"The music's not important, it's the dancing that counts." O'Reilley wondered even as he spoke what compelled him to make remarks that he knew annoyed her. He wondered if it wasn't a sort of behavior he had adopted to deliberately keep himself at a distance from her. If that was the motive, it certainly worked. She was distant and remarkably cool that evening.

"Should have brought my ten-foot pole," O'Reilley muttered to Paul as they went in. Kruger laughed out loud. Ahead of them was a strange assemblage of locals. Tradesmen, the banker, Roger Whiteshead, Hurock and his sons; even old Kraus, who stood uneasily with Pierre Brieux, Captain Hofacker, and a man in a soft gray uniform with twin lightning bolts on his collar. Colonel Olbricht was explaining in a nicely modulated voice that the SD was the security branch of the SS.

O'Reilley drifted nearer, alert for any information of value. But his eyes continued to roam toward the doorway, where the tall cool lady with the auburn hair greeted the arriving guests.

He saw Paul amble toward a bar near the back of the hall and at the same time noticed the other man. He stood there sipping from a glass of wine. His pale eyes fixed admiringly on Ellen. He was a tall man in naval whites with fair hair and even features that were enhanced by a scar across his forehead. The submarine captain, O'Reilley decided.

Olbricht's voice droned on. O'Reilley walked toward the bar himself, saying hello to several people. He saw with annoyance that the submarine captain was still gazing at Ellen.

"Anyone know anything, Pauli?" O'Reilley asked, reaching for the bottle of sherry. What, he wondered, had Gore done with his crystal? Maybe he was afraid of being looted.

"I understand there's to be a speech later. It'll be explained."

And it was, half an hour later, as the last of the guests arrived. There was the tinkling of a bell, and then a silence as Olbricht waited. He looked at the faces around him before speaking.

"I am sure you are wondering why you have been summoned here. To meet me and my friend Captain von Roenne, to be sure. To enjoy a pleasant evening." Olbricht let his mouth slip into a deeply curved frown. "However, there is another matter which is not so pleasant to discuss. This afternoon," he said, his voice rising, "an attempt was made on my life. The attempt failed, obviously!" A nervous wave of laughter followed this apparent joke. "I am, I hope, to be your friend while I stay in the Cameroons. However, I am also a military man, the highest ranking officer of the occupation army. I must do my duty even if it means we cannot be friends.

"This afternoon's assassination attempt was abetted by Europeans!" His voice boomed out suddenly. "This has been proven to my satisfaction by Major Brieux. I must therefore tell you this: The person or persons responsible will be found. And they will be executed. If there is another such incident— well, then perhaps the consequences of that action will fall on all of you, innocent and guilty alike." He shrugged then and smiled faintly, and at that moment O'Reilley decided that if he ever got the opportunity, he would kill Olbricht himself.

Some of those present didn't seem to comprehend what Olbricht was telling them. O'Reilley did. Another attempt on his life, on any German life, any molestation of German property . . . and some of those present, perhaps all of them, would die.

The man moved. Only a finger, but Dr. Henshaw's head snapped up and he bent eagerly over Walther Diels. "Walther, can you hear me?" he asked, reaching for his stethoscope. The eyes that fixed themselves on his face seemed alert, but the heart was very weak.

His hand unexpectedly stretched out and gripped Henshaw's stethoscope like a claw. Henshaw, assuming that the arm and searching hand were randomly groping for any hold on life, gently placed the hand to one side and bent his head to listen intently to the fluttering heartbeat.

Again the hand stretched out and the stethoscope was tugged at. Henshaw frowned, looked into the bright, distant eyes of Walther Diels, and removed the earpieces.

"What is it, Walther?" he asked, bending his head close to the bluish lips of the German. The man said one word quite distinctly and Henshaw frowned. He waited, but Diels could force no more from his ravaged body. Nor would he again. Walther Diels was dead, his eyes fading, his jaw slack, his pulse stilled.

Henshaw worked for a time trying to revive the man, but he knew it was useless. Perhaps in the very best of hospitals, but not here. He straightened up finally with an ache in the small of his back, closed Diels's eyes, and walked to the door, patting at his forehead with a folded handkerchief.

"You'd better call Colonel Olbricht," he told the SS man outside the door.

8

ELLEN HADN'T BEEN telling the truth. There was music issuing from an old gramophone, and dancing. But it wasn't doing O'Reilley much good. She spent her time waltzing with Count von Roenne, to O'Reilley's great annoyance.

Olbricht had left earlier, but now he was back, talking congenially to the locals. There was much mention of sincere hope, deep concern for the well-being of all in the Cameroons.

O'Reilley was on his fourth or fifth glass of wine. The scratchy music from the record player drifted in and out of his consciousness. He found himself near Olbricht, studying the man, listening to the insincere quality of his voice, seeing the beast that lurked behind his solicitous facade.

"And here is our hunter," Lord Gore said.

"Yes?" Olbricht turned to look up at Eric O'Reilley. "A man of guns, are you?"

"When the adversary doesn't have one to fire back," O'Reilley answered quickly, sensing the curiosity behind the casual question. Olbricht was looking for someone. Someone who had armed a native and might consider more action against the Reich.

"I wondered why you were not in the war, a man of your age."

"To fight for what," O'Reilley demanded. "The English?" His brogue thickened considerably. "My grandfather was hanged by the English. As you know, Colonel Olbricht, there's many in Ireland who are on your side in this conflict."

"Yes?" Olbricht wasn't sure if he was buying or not. "And in America? You are an American, are you not?"

"What do we care? Why are we in this war anyway? To save

the British? Lindbergh knew what he was talking about. It's all Roosevelt's doing. Him and international Jewry. I don't want to talk about all of that, though. I'm not a nationalist, so I'm not much of a patriot. I only want it to be over with, and frankly, I don't care much who wins."

Gore looked convincingly incensed, Olbricht amused.

"You have rifles, I assume," the SD officer asked casually. "In your business they are your subsistence, are they not? And yet"—he glanced at Brieux, who stood nearby—"they are illegal just now."

"I didn't say I had any guns," O'Reilley said, staggering a bit, and not only for effect. He winked broadly. "But I'll say this—after you finish your business here, I'll show you some big-game hunting. You'd like that, Colonel. I've got a lion spotted and waiting—world-class head on him, if you're interested."

Olbricht was. They spent some time talking about hunting before O'Reilley drifted away, his pulse racing. He would have preferred planting his fist in the German's face. Kruger wasn't around. O'Reilley wondered if his girl, Nellie, had been invited. If so, they were probably out by the peach trees.

He didn't see Ellen Henshaw either, nor the blond submarine captain, and he moved to the bar, muttering softly to himself.

"It is all right?" Peter Karl Neff, Count von Roenne, asked the slender, auburn-haired woman.

"Yes." Ellen returned to him, and they stood close together on the patio, huge African stars sparkling above. "That is," she sighed, "there's nothing to do. Diels is dead. That's what drew the colonel out of the house. Just now the SS men are tearing the place apart bit by bit, looking for whatever it is they want."

"You do not know what it is?" Roenne asked, almost hopefully. He didn't want this woman involved in anything unhealthy.

"No." Ellen turned to face him, to look up into the handsome, slightly haughty, slightly weary face of this German aristocrat. "Do you, Count von Roenne?"

"No—please call me Peter—I have no idea." He sipped at his sherry, looking through the trees toward the moonlit face of the sea.

"But you brought them here!" Ellen said with polite disbelief.

"Yes, but I do not know what they want. It's not a military secret I'm keeping, Ellen. Some sort of intelligence information, of course, but I have no idea what. After all, the Cameroons are hardly what one would suppose to be a critical area. I do know this—if you people know what it is, to deny it to Olbricht could be very bad."

"Yes," she said, moving still nearer to von Roenne.

"Very bad," he emphasized. "These SS people are filth, Ellen. For that alone," he said with a sardonic smile, "I could be shot. Nevertheless, it is true." He hesitated, then took her by the hand and led her to the little marble bench beside the patio balustrade. Sitting her down, he told her more about Olbricht and the death of Lieutenant Holzlohner.

"But that's terrible!" Ellen exclaimed.

"Yes. Of course it is terrible; much is terrible in Germany just now."

"Then you are not . . . ," her hand briefly covered his, "a patriot?"

"You misunderstand me. Of course I am a patriot. I am, more importantly, a warrior. I have taken an oath to my country, an oath to this Hitler." Von Roenne's mouth turned down.

"But if what your country asks is wrong—"

"If it is, then I will do what is wrong," von Roenne said and Ellen sat staring at the man by starlight, wondering at the Germans, at a country that could produce great thinkers, musicians, artists, and yet, beneath its tradition of fine culture, be a nation of barbarians.

"I cannot argue with such logic," she said stiffly.

"No," von Roenne said with a smile, "for it is not logic. They say we are a mystical race—perhaps so. But I would die,

I assure you, before I would break my oath." The woman was drawing away from him, von Roenne saw, not physically, but emotionally. "It sounds terrible to you, I know that. I think, however, if I were an Englishman who had said the same thing, you would applaud me."

"No Englishman," Ellen said a little woodenly, "would ever be asked to do some of the things a German soldier does."

"Perhaps not." Von Roenne shrugged and lit a cigarette, taking a deep drag. "Truthfully, I do not know how much of what one hears is true. There are always horror stories during war, as you know. I have seen some propaganda films that clothe the British in malignity. All of us in Germany saw many of these in the thirties. Is there some truth? Only a little? None? Who knows. I have spent the war in my own vessel, beneath the sea. I have done my work. For the rest of it I know nothing."

"And care nothing?" Ellen asked heatedly. How could anyone be as cool and insensitive as this man?

"The time for caring has gone," von Roenne said. "Perhaps it will come again, I do not know. There is no time for moral considerations in war. I have killed. I will probably kill again. If I do, I shall be rewarded again—you see, the morality becomes inverted. Well," he said as he stood, "I see you do not care for this. I have, I am afraid, lost any fascination I might have had for you, and that, Ellen, sorrows me. You are a fine and proud young woman. Intelligent and, as you realize, most beautiful. Your young man is very fortunate. I almost wish I were he."

"What young man?" Ellen asked, still dazed by von Roenne's views.

"This O'Reilley," von Roenne said, helping Ellen up. Holding her hand briefly.

"O'Reilley!" Ellen laughed loudly. "You misunderstand, Count von Roenne. He and I have nothing whatever in common. He cares for nothing but himself. He is a butcher of animals—"

"And not a butcher of men?" Roenne asked with a sad smile. "Well, perhaps I am wrong. About your feelings toward him.

Yet each time I looked at this man tonight, I saw him gazing at you, and when we danced his eyes were daggers against me. No, whatever you feel about him, Miss Henshaw, this man is in love with you."

The idea astonished Ellen. She thought about O'Reilley—tall, strong, outspoken, crude—and she almost laughed. Almost, but she did not. Roenne offered her his arm, and they walked back into the hall where the thinning crowd still stood drinking, speaking in low tones, watching a few dancers. O'Reilley was there, and his eyes sparked across the room. Von Roenne noticed it as well. He bent down and whispered into Ellen's ear, "You see? The man is madly in love with you, Ellen, and if we do not part—although I would do so with deep regret—I am afraid I shall have to fight this wild-eyed Irishman. And I was taught very early not to duel with a man who has made weapons a way of life."

He kissed her lightly on the forehead, bowed, and strode away toward the cloakroom while O'Reilley stood glaring; and Ellen, confused by a new swirl of emotions, smiled with something close to pleasure.

Lord Gore touched O'Reilley's elbow as the hunter blearily contemplated the submarine officer. "Eric, please come to my study."

O'Reilley glanced at Lord Gore, then searched the room briefly. When he saw that Brieux, Hofacker, and Olbricht all seemed to be absent, he nodded.

"Five minutes," Gore added.

Paul Kruger reappeared, looking satisfied. He poured a glass of wine and said, "Everything all right?"

"Yes."

"You look like hell. No night to get drunk, Eric."

"Who's getting drunk?" O'Reilley demanded belligerently.

Kruger shrugged and turned his back so that O'Reilley wouldn't see the smile on his lips.

"I'm going up to Gore's study. Keep an eye out, will you?"

"Sure." Kruger was still smiling as O'Reilley moved unsteadily away. Paul wasn't the only one watching the American.

Looking across the room, Paul saw Ellen Henshaw surreptitiously glancing that way as she spoke to Roger Whiteshead. Paul Kruger had a small contented sound beneath his breath and filled his glass again.

O'Reilley found Lord Gore in his study with Dr. Henshaw. Both men were smoking cigars.

"Anyone out there, Eric?"

"No, sir. They're all gone somewhere."

"Next-door. They're demolishing the Diels house."

"Looking for what?"

"I've no idea at all. But we may know where it is."

O'Reilley's head came up with amazement.

"That is," Gore added, "we have a clue as to where it might be. I can't make sense out of it at the moment, and neither can Dr. Henshaw."

"What sort of clue?" Eric asked, roaming the room. He straightened a plaster Venus de Milo on the mantel.

"Diels spoke one word before he passed away. The word," Gore said apologetically, "was *Hünchen*."

"It sounded like *Hünchen*," Dr. Henshaw quickly corrected.

"I don't speak German," O'Reilley reminded them. "What does it mean?"

"I'm not sure that's what he said," Henshaw repeated.

"It means 'chicken,' Eric," Gore provided. "A man's name, a place, a code word, or a completely irrelevant dying thought— we have no idea which it was."

"I am not certain that was the word," Henshaw said again, emphatically.

"All right. It may have been, perhaps not," O'Reilley said. "You two may be able to come up with a German word that sounds like that. It may mean something. It makes no difference, does it? It makes no difference if we find whatever it is Olbricht is looking for."

"Of course it does," Henshaw said stiffly. "If we had it, we could give it to the man and he would go away."

"It would be best to get rid of him," Lord Gore agreed.

"Would it?" O'Reilley turned to face them both. "Hasn't it

90

occurred to you that anything Olbricht was sent this far to get might be important?"

"Of course, but . . ." Lord Gore faltered.

"Or have we given up the idea of resistance?"

"At what cost?" Henshaw demanded. "We haven't a chance as things stand, and everyone knows it. The personal objective in wartime is simply to survive, O'Reilley. That is the objective of all of us in Douala."

"You included."

"Do you think I want to see Ellen thrown into a labor camp?"

"No." O'Reilley shook his head. Was he, then, wrong? There was no one left who had the stomach for this. "What about Brieux?" he asked with little hope.

"His position has not altered," Lord Gore said.

"Then we're going to try to ride it out?"

"Yes."

"Hasn't it occurred to you gentlemen that we may not be able to?" O'Reilley leaned intently forward. "If Olbricht doesn't find what he wants, he's going to search the town. He's already got SS patrols in the streets. He's already destroyed a Bamileke village. It will get worse, gentlemen."

"And so we must help him find what he wants!" Henshaw shouted.

"You help him," O'Reilley said. For a moment, he simply stood looking at them, and then he abruptly turned and walked out the door, slamming it shut behind him.

"For God's sake," Henshaw muttered, "you'd think this was Poland." Gore didn't answer. He wasn't sure about many things. On the one hand stood battle and death, thefruits of war; on the other—perhaps death without battle? He only wished that Olbricht had never come to the Cameroons. For of one thing he was certain: Olbricht would have his way, or blood would run in the streets of Douala.

"What's up?" Kruger asked as Eric strode toward him.

"Nothing's up. Everyone's buckling."

"Well, that's all we ever expected."

"Yes."

"Makes a man feel like thinking about rafting to Mbandaka, doesn't it?"

"Yes, and next year we can fight them there." He started toward the door, still fuming, and Kruger fell in beside him.

Outside it was still and dark. The moon cast a faint, pale haze upon the eastern sky. Vervets shrilled in the treetops. The black youth stepped out of the bushes and motioned frantically. O'Reilley recognized Tami immediately. He was Mesotho's oldest son, a twelve-year-old with long gangly limbs, a ready smile, and a sharp mind. He was afflicted with boils, which Mesotho refused to allow Dr. Henshaw to treat.

"What is it?"

The boy's hand rested on O'Reilley's arm. "They have him again. Big soldiers."

"They have Mesotho?"

"Yes," Tami said gloomily. He brightened. "But you will bring him home again."

"Where is he, Tami?" Kruger asked.

"At the gold mine. In the camp."

"Damn," O'Reilley breathed. Snatching Mesotho away from Brieux's lethargic legionnaires hadn't been much of a job, but getting in and out of Hofacker's labor camp wasn't remotely similar. Undoubtedly, there would be SS men there as well, and if Olbricht had the notion that Mesotho was behind the assassination attempt, it could already be too late to save the Bamileke chief.

Michelle slept uneasily beside him. O'Reilley, hands clasped behind his head, stared at the ceiling. He turned his head, looking at her childlike sleeping face, at the smudge of makeup below her eye, the smooth pale shoulder.

Suddenly he sat bolt upright, his head spinning with the abrupt motion, his pulse lifting. He had an idea—perhaps a substanceless notion, but he couldn't say. An idea that had to be pursued.

Hünchen. Why should Diels have spoken of chickens at the moment of his death unless it had been very important to him?

O'Reilley had been to the Diels's house once, for one of those holiday parties, and as he stalked Ellen Henshaw without success, he had detected a familiar odor drifting through the night. Diels had been with him and had laughed when he mentioned it. "One day I must have that taken away—there's an old chicken coop down there. I thought of using the fertilizer on the flowers, but Frau Diels insists it is too strong."

O'Reilley hesitated briefly, then slid from the bed and started to dress. Tying his bootlaces, he took the Beretta from its hiding place, glanced back at the sleeping woman, and slipped out.

The streets were far from empty. He saw three patrolling men in the first two blocks—two French legionnaires and one heavily armed SS man. The moon was riding high in the inky sky, illuminating the dusty breadth of Prince Edward Boulevard. O'Reilley went down the alley beside the Bank of England and slipped through the cluttered alley behind it, nearly stumbling over a snoring Bamileke curled around his bottle of rum.

It wasn't quite sane, he told himself, to risk getting killed for a glimpse of an old chicken house. Yet the notion that it was important, that it *had* to be important, overrode his doubts.

Once into the trees beyond the wharf road, he moved with confident ease. O'Reilley had spent half of his adult life in the jungle stalking creatures far more alert and just as dangerous as an SS man.

Suddenly he hit the ground, wriggling forward on his belly into a thicker clump of brush. The flashlight flickered from side to side as the two soldiers moved along the path between the Diels house and the governor's mansion. O'Reilley felt the perspiration track down his cheek, felt the sharp-edged grass scraping his face. He could see two pairs of high boots now, see the moonlight reflecting off the highly polished leather and off the dull blue muzzle of an automatic weapon.

He pressed himself closer to the ground, his hand cramping around the butt of his handgun, which would be next to useless if they spotted him.

They stopped directly before him, a few meters away, and

lit cigarettes, discussing someone far away in time and place who had dropped her fans in the middle of her dance. They smoked endlessly. O'Reilley's body was numb with tension, but finally they strode away, their boots crushing gravel.

Looking across the expanse of yard he could make out still other troops. They had the house ringed, and if he had any sense, he thought, he would just withdraw now. He moved forward, banking on the fact that he did not want to penetrate to the house, where their forces were concentrated, but only to the back yard where he thought they would not be as attentive. But there were two men at the back of the house, moving in silent round, one man farther down, not fifty feet from the henhouse itself, his flashlight idly searching the bushes from time to time as he sat on a stone wall, his heels tapping against it.

O'Reilley's heart was racing. Perspiration stung his eyes. The gun in his hand seemed very small. He waited until the guard on the walk above him had turned and started back, and then he went forward again, moving in a crouch. The guard's flashlight painted a pale circle in the area of the henhouse, then moved toward the trees. The soldier's eyes were following the beam of light and not the progress of the shadow that scurried along the base of the six-foot-high stone wall.

He felt the sharp, strong tug at his ankles, felt the world fall away from him. His neck cracked against the stone, and he fell to the ground with a muffled thud.

O'Reilley stuffed a handkerchief into the guard's mouth, stripped his body of weapons, rolled him onto his face and strapped the man's belt around his wrists in a figure-eight.

After crouching silently, listening to the night sounds, O'Reilley moved on. The chicken coop was musty and dark. An unlikely place to hide anything, he thought as he crept in the ill-fitting door. Maybe that was why it had been chosen by Diels. Unless this was all some sort of opium dream, a nightmare notion. What could Diels have that was so important to the SS anyway? He had heavy doubts about all of this.

He ran a hand along the shelving inside the shack, disturbing

94

the bats and spiders that clustered among the old, ruptured feed sacks. Then he probed the floor with a rusted pitchfork but found no loose soil. Finally he thrust it into the pile of manure itself. Manure left by generations of hens, indicating the careless husbandry of the original owner. O'Reilley frowned. The stuff should have been more compacted, with a crust. He glanced toward the door, wondering how long it would be before they noticed the other guard was missing.

He was nearly ready to give it up and get the hell out of there when the tines struck something with a metallic thunk, and in seconds, digging furiously with his hands, O'Reilley had uncovered the steel box.

Setting it aside with trembling hands, he tried to cover his tracks as best he could, smoothing the manure down, wiping his footprints out with his hands as he crawled out, dragging the box with him.

Then he was in the moonlit yard again, moving back toward the wall.

The dark figure loomed up suddenly before O'Reilley, and with the reflexes of a cat he leaped. As their bodies collided he already knew he'd made a mistake.

The wind rushed out of Ellen Henshaw's body as she hit the ground, O'Reilley's body pressed against hers, his hand clamped over her mouth. Beyond the wall, men were moving around, speaking in low voices. Once O'Reilley heard the distinct, chilling sound of a weapon being cocked there was nothing to do but lie there, Ellen beneath him, his body pressed against her sleek length.

She wore only a light wrapper, which had fallen open, and a thin, white negligee beneath, against which her breasts rose and fell irregularly. Another woman might have struggled, but she seemed to take in the situation instantly. She had no fear of O'Reilley, perhaps only contempt. As he moved his hand slowly away from her mouth she made no attempt to speak. When at last O'Reilley drew away, the box under his arm, she got to her knees. The moonlight spilled through the peach trees, and even at this moment he was struck by her beauty. Her auburn hair was loose around her shoulders, an errant strand flowing across her breasts, which were milk white, smooth, unrestricted beneath the white negligee. Her eyes, however, were mocking.

O'Reilley jerked her to her feet with more violence than was necessary. He stood holding her arm, and she stared at him calmly. There was a muffled exclamation from beyond the wall, and Ellen stood on tiptoe to whisper. "This way. Father's laboratory."

Then she yanked her arm out of his grasp and moved swiftly toward a small outbuilding with a tiled roof, tying her wrapper as they went. Now the lights were blazing in the Diels's house and O'Reilley could hear a truck arriving. A whistle sounded twice and was answered.

Ellen took a key from her pocket and opened the door to the small building. After they went in, she locked the door and sagged to the floor. O'Reilley sat beside her, the box on his lap, her scent in his nostrils, her hand only inches from his, though her body and thoughts seemed miles away.

They sat that way for a long time while the moon rose high and the excitement near the Diels house died away.

"Well, Mr. O'Reilley," Ellen said at last. "It has been interesting watching you stir up trouble, but I'm exhausted and I'd like to go to bed. Would you like to tell me first what this is all—"

She started to rise, but O'Reilley's hand stretched out and yanked her down. She lost her composure briefly, her eyes growing wide and frightened as she, too, heard the footsteps outside, the rattle of the doorknob. It was another moment before Dr. Henshaw came in and turned on the lights, as Ellen pushed away from O'Reilley with disgust and embarrassment.

"Pardon me!" Dr. Henshaw said, gaping at his daughter, dishabille in the arms of a stranger on the floor of his laboratory. "I just wanted to get something. I had no idea—"

"Really, Father," Ellen said, tearing herself away from O'Reilley. "How could you imagine such a thing. With O'Reilley!" She laughed, and O'Reilley's jaw tightened. "I thought I heard something near the old chicken coop and I came out to see what it was, and found him."

"What then?" Henshaw asked with some anxiety. "Has this anything to do with the injured man next door?"

"Yes, as a matter of fact," O'Reilley said, getting to his feet, holding the box under his arm. Henshaw narrowed his gaze. "May I ask what that is? It isn't . . . !" His breath was sucked in sharply. When he spoke again, it was more of a dry croak than human speech. "It isn't what they're looking for, is it, O'Reilley?"

"I think it is. We can't open it here, though."

"Why not? I work here every night. Nothing unusual at all about the lights being on."

O'Reilley looked around the room, which was bisected by a long white table cluttered with scientific instruments. "All right," he agreed, "but I think Lord Gore ought to be here too."

"I'll get him," the doctor volunteered. "Ellen, perhaps you'd better return to bed."

"After what I've been through? Not likely, Father. I'll stay. Go on. I'll chance it a little while longer with the Irish ruffian."

A dozen rejoinders sprang into Eric's mind; none of them, fortunately, found their way to his lips. He turned a wooden chair with a low back around and sat down, facing the workbench, the steel box before him.

It was another ten minutes before Lord Gore appeared, wearing his robe. The doctor was right on his heels. "Is that it?" Gore asked.

"It appears to be. I haven't opened it yet."

"Let's do so, Eric. Open it."

"Perhaps we shouldn't," said Dr. Henshaw. "I mean, perhaps we should just deliver it to Olbricht without looking."

"To Olbricht?" O'Reilley's voice was low and gravelly.

"Yes—after all, it does belong to them. If he gets what he came for, he'll leave and we'll all be out of danger."

"We don't know if this is what he came for, Michael," Gore pointed out. "Until we have a look."

"No, that's true. No sense making fools out of ourselves."

O'Reilley was still staring at the doctor, and at Ellen, who stood beside him, apparently sharing his point of view.

"We'll have our look then, Eric," Gore said calmly. "Then we'll discuss it."

"I won't give it to them," O'Reilley said. "Not if it's something our side can use."

"Our side!" Ellen exploded. "Our side—you and a hundred black Africans? Our side! We only want to be done with the war, Eric O'Reilley. That's what *our* side wants. To get this man Olbricht out of here before anyone else is hurt."

O'Reilley didn't respond. He jimmied the box open and sat staring at a sheet of paper. He glanced at the others and handed them each a folder, and in that small, primitive laboratory in the equatorial country of the Cameroons, they discovered what the war was about.

9

O'Reilley shifted nearer to the lamp. The others still silently scanned their reports with various degrees of amazement. O'Reilley began to read his out loud.

"We have large collections of skulls of almost all races, however we could use representative samples of the subhuman Jew. Following the induced death of the Jew, whose head should not be damaged, sever the head and forward it in a hermetically sealed can. Fifty specimens should be sufficient for this experiment."

Ellen Henshaw cleared her throat and read slowly, her face growing ashen. "The third test was given without oxygen at a simulated altitude of thirty-seven thousand feet. Respiration continued for twenty minutes. After the thirtieth minute, the inhalations ceased."

And Lord Gore: "All prisoners with tattooing on them should report to the dispensary. The most artistic specimens are to be killed by injection, and the skins detached from the bodies."

And finally Dr. Henshaw, his hand trembling, read a weekly report from Dachau. "Still another improvement made here is that at Treblinka the victims almost always knew they were to be exterminated. Here we fool the victims into thinking they are to be deloused. Of course sometimes they realize our intentions and we have riots and difficulties. Very frequently women try to hide their children under the clothes they remove, but of course we always find them. Our semiannual total now stands at seventy-six thousand Jews, Bolsheviks, and other subhumans exterminated."

There was more, but he couldn't go on. He buried his face in his hands as Ellen stood staring at O'Reilley, who was placing file after file on the table, including some from manufacturers of ovens and gas chambers touting their wares; an inventory of the tons of hair obtained for mattress stuffing, a folder marked SECRET reporting the amount of gold ripped from the teeth of exterminated prisoners.

And among the papers was the signed order, the one with the hated name scrawled across its bottom. *This shall be done*, it said, *because it is ordered so, by: A. Hitler, Deine Führer.*

O'Reilley looked at Henshaw and demanded, "Well! Shall we take this over and give it to Olbricht now?"

Henshaw only shook his head. It was a minute before he could answer. "I didn't know. How could anyone guess? Turn it over to them?" he said, his head coming up so that O'Reilley could see the tears in the doctor's eyes. "Give me a gun, O'Reilley. I have seen all I want to see of the New Order."

Lord Gore was more rational. "Yes," he said, "that's very fine to say, Henshaw, but the fact is we can't do very much at all, and if we try . . . well, you've just seen what they're capable of."

"Still, we have to do something."

"Yes," Gore said, "I suppose so. O'Reilley? You've been working on this for a while—what should we do?"

"The first thing to do is get out of here, out of your house and out of Douala." Tonight we were lucky. They figured the guard fell. Maybe tomorrow he'll remember differently when the concussion wears off. Perhaps Olbricht will have a different idea when the report gets to him."

"We can't run off, man!" Gore said, as if O'Reilley had suggested flying to the moon.

"Yes, you can, and you'd better. I'm going to try to get Mesotho out of their hands again. Failing that, I'm going to talk to the Bamilekes anyway and see if they'll still fight. Once that starts, there won't be any safe place in Douala." He added, "Besides, we can't keep the papers here."

"But where?" Henshaw asked.

"There's the Dutchman's house. That's what Kruger and I

were going to use. Olbricht won't know of it, nor I think will Brieux. It's been abandoned for years."

"That's fifteen miles out."

"Yes. I've got to make some arrangements in town. It won't take more than an hour. Then I'll be back with Sal Hurock's truck. His gas gauge always reads empty, but the old sinner has another tank that's not on the gauge. He's got a storage tank at his house that he's been filling up from at night for years."

"And he would lend it to us?" Ellen asked.

"I don't recall saying I was going to borrow it. I'll be back in an hour. Not to here, but down along the beach road."

Things were moving too fast for the others. They had a dozen objections, but none of them had much substance. "There's Frau Diels," Henshaw remembered. "She's staying over here. I've got her on a sedative."

"All right, bring her, too. Better have the servants take to the bush."

"What about the others—the rest of the townspeople, O'Reilley? My God, we're dooming them!"

"Maybe. But we can't help prevent that if we're dead. This is the best plan I can come up with. If you've another, let's hear it now." Following their silence, Eric said, "All right. We'll proceed as discussed. Bring all the food and water you can carry. Fill some burlap sacks with canned goods. Doctor, you'd better make sure you have your bag."

There wasn't any time for further conversation. Ellen was looking at him oddly as he left. Henshaw still seemed dazed, and Gore appeared intent on maintaining his nerve but was having a tough time of it.

O'Reilley slipped away through the trees. The ground was moon-pooled. Once, far away, Eric thought he heard a leopard roar, but it might have been a truck starting up, or the blood rushing in his ears.

Uptown there was a lot more activity than there should have been. French patrols were out, and O'Reilley saw at least one

SS man. He could see the Europa on his right now. Beyond, the sea sparkled darkly in the moonlight.

The cry from an alleyway beyond the cabaret caused O'Reilley to break into a run. His boots rang off the stones of the street. Rounding the corner of the alley, he came face to face with a German soldier. O'Reilley brought his forearm up under the soldier's chin and heard the crackle of torn gristle, the snap of bone. The German slumped to the alley. Beyond the soldier was Paul Kruger, and in front of him another dead soldier, his blood staining the alley darkly. In front of Kruger a small dark form lay sprawled.

O'Reilley stepped forward. "Paul, it's me."

Kruger had been crouched and ready, his pistol starting to track upward until he recognized his friend. At that moment O'Reilley decided that Kruger was a very dangerous man. There was a ferocity in his eyes, a determination O'Reilley hadn't seen before.

"What's happened?"

"Damned Krauts were after the kid," Kruger said savagely.

"Tami?"

It was Mesotho's boy, and it looked as if he was hurt. Tami moaned and Kruger turned to him. O'Reilly crouched beside Kruger to examine the boy. He seemed bewildered, but not seriously injured. Briefly, O'Reilley told Kruger about what had happened that evening in Henshaw's laboratory and about their plan.

"All right. That's all fine, but I'm not leaving Tami."

O'Reilley looked in puzzlement at his friend, then smiled in the darkness. "No need to. I'm going to hook Hurock's truck if I can. Where are the guns?"

"In the loft in the Africa-West."

Africa-West was another casualty of the war, a once-flourishing export organization where Kruger and O'Reilley had sold many of their wares.

"All right, can you get them?"

"He'll be all right here," Paul said. "Like I said, I want my Mannlicher." This weapon was a .458 capable of shooting completely through an engine block or a mad elephant and which Paul Kruger could fire six times in as many seconds with uncanny accuracy.

"I'll get the truck if I can." There was more motor traffic on the boulevard as Germans investigated the shots. Now they would be after Kruger and O'Reilley, and if they wanted to, they could hold the hunters indefinitely for carrying pistols. "I'll pick up Michelle and get back here as soon as I can."

"No."

"No, what?"

"Don't try to get Michelle, Eric. They've got her. Or at least they're watching her. She gave me over to them."

"What are you talking about?" O'Reilley felt mingled rage and dread rising. He stepped nearer to Kruger, seeing Paul's eyes flicker uneasily.

"I'm talking about Michelle, damn it. I'd moved out of the hotel tonight. I was holed up in the back rooms at the Brittania Company Store, waiting for you. I wanted to stay off the streets, all right? But I had to leave word for you, so I told Michelle, and only Michelle, where I'd be. Two hours ago three SS men broke into the old store and marched right to my door."

"What happened?"

"What the hell do you think? I'm here."

"It had to be Michelle? You're sure?"

"Sure, Eric."

"Then they have her."

"Maybe."

Eric flared up angrily. "What do you mean, 'maybe'? Why else would she talk?"

"I don't know, Eric." He rested a hand on O'Reilley's shoulder briefly. "Maybe you do. Let's get moving, though. I don't suppose I can talk you out of going for her."

"No. Get the guns." He looked around the deserted dock, seeing the German submarine far across the bay, the rotting fishing nets, the broken-down river patrol boat. "Maybe you'd better move Tami into the warehouse."

"All right."

"Did he say anything to you?"

"In that pileup? You must be kidding," Kruger replied. "He's been keeping an eye out for his father. Olbricht's taken him somewhere, and it's not Victoria. That could be what he came for."

"Likely," O'Reilley said. "I hope that's it. We need Mesotho badly."

"If the Krauts have him, it won't be so easy to get him back."

"No. I don't expect it to be."

Kruger was crouched down now too, his hand resting on Tami's heaving chest. "You like this one, don't you?" Eric asked.

Kruger growled, "Yeah, a little fighter, he is."

"Sure." O'Reilley said his good-bye and moved off down the docks as Kruger picked up the boy and made his way toward the deserted warehouse. God help anyone who tries to take him, O'Reilley thought. It would take an army against Paul and his Mannlicher.

O'Reilley twice spotted African patrols and once a German motorcycle sputtering and popping past, the man in the sidecar carrying a machine gun, but he still reached the Hurock family's boat shed in fifteen minutes. The door was locked, but the window had been left open. Eric lifted himself up and over the sill and, moving cautiously in the near-darkness, found the truck parked between two trailer-mounted boats.

He got the truck started by crossing the wires, and the old Ford V-8 roared to life. Dropping it into low gear, he got the ungainly one-ton truck into motion. He eased the front bumper up against the double doors and nudged the throttle until, with a creaking and moaning, the lock popped and the truck was free to roll through the night streets of Douala.

Making his way through the alleys, he pulled up behind the Europa, yanking the ignition wires apart. The engine rattled to a stop, and Eric, checking the Beretta, climbed out and went in the back door.

Music came to his ears: sweet and low, Madame Valery's favorite blues record. There was a band of light beneath Michelle's door and he walked over, then placed his ear next to the door. He heard nothing but Michelle, humming to the distant music. She would be swaying as she always did, one hand on her hip, her head thrown slightly back. O'Reilley tried the door. It was unlocked, and he pushed on through.

The SS man was naked, frightened, stunned to immobility. O'Reilley, who had been expecting almost anything, managed to move first. Leaping forward, he clubbed down with his Beretta, splitting the scalp of the German, putting out his lights.

The SS man slumped forward across the bed, then slowly slid onto the floor, a worm of blood trickling down across his eye.

Michelle stood naked, hands on hips, hair across one eye, her face scornful and yet composed. "Jealous?" she asked, her eyelids half-lowered, her lower lip thrust aggressively forward.

"Michelle." He just looked at her, feeling the frustration rise. She had reduced war, life, and death to the level of a lover's quarrel. She was behaving as if they were both in Paris, not understanding that she had given Kruger and himself over to a savage enemy.

"What are you doing here, Eric? Go away, go back to your English woman."

"That's what I'm going to do." O'Reilley found her cotton dress across the chair and flung it at her. "You're coming along."

"No. Why should I?" She kicked at her dress petulantly.

"Don't you have any understanding of what is going on here?" he shouted, gripping her arms so tightly that his fingers dug into her smooth flesh, whitening it. "They'll have you down at police headquarters or worse."

"Why?" she asked, her eyes calm, too calm.

"Because," Eric explained with parental patience, "this man has been hurt. I was here. I'm wanted, don't you see?"

Blithely she said, "It has nothing to do with me. They don't hurt women. So they lock you up for a few weeks; maybe that will give you time to think about Michelle and what she has done for you, eh?"

"Michelle—" He took a step forward, but she sidestepped

him, her eyes annoyingly mischievous, and before O'Reilley could stop her she had ducked under his arm and was out in the hall, pulling on her robe as she ran. He could hear her voice.

"Oh, soldier, soldier! He's here."

O'Reilley's head exploded with tiny red flares. Was she mad? No one could be that vengeful. He saw the SS man's automatic weapon, picked it up, and stepped into the dimly lighted hall. He heard Michelle's chatting voice, heard the pounding of boots as the SS soldiers burst into the hall. Michelle was behind them, breathless, laughing. Until the Germans cut loose with automatic weapons fire. Bullets tore into the wooden walls, gouging out large splinters as the staccato roar of the guns deafened O'Reilley. With Michelle there, he couldn't fire back. He saw the awe and terror wash out the amusement on her face. Then he dove for the outer door behind him, bullets punching through it after him.

He was into the garden and over the fence before the SS men, confident of a kill, burst through the door. They were backlighted, their silhouettes stark and heavy. O'Reilley flicked the trigger of the submachine gun in his hands and watched as the weapon spat flame and death at the door of the Europa. One of the men was slammed back against the wall, his rifle clattering free, his head half-severed. The second dove for the shelter of the hallway behind him, but O'Reilley's fire raked his legs and he lay still, a horrified scream rising from his throat.

O'Reilley didn't wait to see anymore. He ran to the truck and wired it with trembling fingers, the machine gun beside him on the seat. The starter balked and O'Reilley cursed. He tried it again and the truck roared to life. Jamming it into gear, he rumbled down the alley, holding the throttle flat against the floor, the lights out. A gang of German soldiers, guns in hand, appeared directly before him and then scattered as the massive whining truck raced through them. There was one solid thud, a muffled cry of pain, and then O'Reilley was out of the alley, cranking the wheel hard to circle back toward the docks.

His lights were still switched off, but the moon showed the

road clearly enough. He hit the horn three times before braking to a stop in front of the Africa-West.

Kruger was already in motion. He came forward at a run with the cases containing their hunting equipment and tossed them over the tailgate. He was still running when he returned to the building to get Tami and two more cases.

In seconds, the African was in the back lying on a bed of fishnets and Kruger was leaping in beside O'Reilley, slamming the tinny door as the Ford surged forward again. From uptown sirens sang, and once there was a shot. A signal or a mistake— or Michelle. . . .

O'Reilley drove demonically, his eyes fixed on the dark road. He flew through the docks, scattering pedestrians. Then they were onto the beach road, seeing the white lines of surf break free of the dark sea as they strung out along the rugged coastline.

"What happened?" Kruger asked him.

"Later."

"Will they be ready?"

"If they're not, we'll have to keep going. I hope to God they're ready."

O'Reilley flicked his headlights on and off as he approached the bend in the road where Lord Gore and the Henshaws would have had to come down the bluff to the road. There was nothing for a moment, and then a small dark figure leaped from the trees, waving its arms. It was Ellen. O'Reilley slammed on the brakes.

"Get in. Now!" O'Reilley commanded, and she turned away at once. In a moment she was back, carrying two gunnysacks. Gore was there, wearing bush khakis, and Henshaw right behind him, in jeans and a cotton shirt. He was assisting someone toward the truck. It was Frau Diels, who appeared shaken or sedated, perhaps both.

Gore climbed into the front, peering back through the small window into the bed of the truck. "They're aboard," he said, and O'Reilley pressed the foot-feed to the floor once more and set off up the dusty, rutted road for the Konjanga turnoff. He thought again of Michelle and cursed loudly, once violently, slamming the heel of his hand into the steering wheel. Then he settled down, concentrated on the jungle as it flickered past on either side, and on the rugged, winding road that the jolting headlights revealed.

At sunrise they were still in the truck, creeping along the goat track that followed the Konjanga River into the uplands. O'Reilley's eyes felt gritty, his hands cramped. The road, which hadn't been maintained since the Dutchman had been lost— killed by wild animals or murdered by natives fifteen years earlier—wound higher. O'Reilley stayed in low gear, creeping up along the washed-out road, his outside wheels perilously close to the edge of a hundred-foot drop. Below ran the Konjanga, which wasn't even enough of a river to be sketched on most maps, but which ran swiftly now, white water spuming into the air.

Finally they were up onto the flats, where no road was necessary. Ahead sat the Dutchman's gabled house. O'Reilley worked his way up through the gears, scattering roaming vervet monkeys and antelope. The vervets, characteristically unafraid of humans, ran away screeching, their greenish-gray fur rippling across their backs. A single male mandrill stared at them belligerently before turning its red rump and loping away.

"Seems well situated," Lord Gore said, the first words spoken since he had climbed aboard. "I've never been out here, nearly forgotten entirely that it existed. Big house. What was the man thinking of?"

No one answered. O'Reilley studied the house as they jounced toward it. Two stories, clapboard, once white. It faced the empty veldt, and at its back rose jungle-clad bluff. It would be simple to spot approaching enemies and, if any were seen, to escape into the tangle of ravines and jungle growth behind.

O'Reilley drove around to the back. They came upon a barn with blistered paint that stood beneath two tall ebony trees, around which strangler figs grew. Kruger jumped out and swung open the double doors to the Dutchman's barn; O'Reilley pulled into its musty interior and stopped the engine, which died with a rattle and a wheeze.

Kruger saw something suspiciously like a Naja cobra slithering toward a collection of junk in the corner of the barn, but he didn't stop to worry about it.

By the time O'Reilley climbed out, they had lowered the tailgate. Frau Diels, still looking dazed, and Doctor Henshaw climbed out. Now they stretched out their hands to take hold of Tami, who didn't look well at all. Henshaw muttered something as he took the boy in his arms and started carrying him toward the house, where Paul Kruger had already opened the back door and was now moving through, looking for unwelcome wildlife.

Lord Gore took the two burlap sacks from Ellen and followed. O'Reilley got the last sack, slung it over his shoulder, and waited while Ellen clambered down. She wore a dark brown skirt and a white, long-sleeved blouse. Her hair was cinched back simply in a leather ring. She seemed about to say something but never got it out.

O'Reilley took her arm and she hopped down. He closed the door behind them and stood scowling, looking out across the dry-grass plains toward Douala.

Inside the house bats, owls, monkeys had made a mess of things. Ellen's nose wrinkled at the sights and smells.

"I hope you brought a broom," Kruger said.

"I saw the remains of one outside," Ellen answered almost cheerfully. She placed her sack on the floor beside the others and went out to fetch it.

Kruger was leaning against the jamb of the kitchen door.

"How's Tami?" O'Reilley asked.

"Not good."

Peering in, O'Reilley saw the doctor laboring over the boy, who had been placed on the dining-room table. Lord Gore stood by, looking worried and ineffectual. Frau Diels had sagged into a dust-covered plush chair.

"Found it!" Ellen said, and again her voice had an unaccustomed light tone. She walked by the two men, her tread light.

"What's up with her?" Eric muttered. He watched her until she was around the corner and out of sight, until they heard Tami give a low groan as the doctor probed.

"I'll get the guns," O'Reilley said gruffly. Kruger was smiling. He was still smiling when O'Reilley went out, slamming the badly hung screen door.

"What's the matter with him?" Ellen asked. She had the broom handle propped against her side and was tying a scarf around her hair.

"Bad times for Eric, that's all. Last night Michelle turned him in. You know, the French girl."

"Turned him in? You mean to the Germans?"

"Exactly."

"But why?" Ellen's fingers had stopped trying to knot the scarf. She stood staring at the back door, at the bright rectangle of sunlight framed by the tattered screen. "I thought they were . . . you know, close."

"They were." Kruger yawned. "She found out that Eric was in love with you."

"She actually thought that?"

"Yes." Kruger pushed himself away from the wall. "Oh, well, but then so does Eric."

With that he began whistling, clearing the kitchen table off for a place to clean and oil the rifles. When O'Reilley came back, submachine gun slung over his shoulder, gun cases in hand, Ellen was standing there gawking at him. Again her mouth opened, again she said nothing. Her father's voice called out from the other room. She turned and left with obvious relief.

"What have you been doing to that woman, Paul?" O'Reilley asked, placing the guns down on the table.

"Nothing at all, my friend. Absolutely nothing."

Kruger's .458 Mannlicher and O'Reilley's .378 Weatherby lay side by side against the table. In addition they had a .303 carbine and the thunder gun, the big .500 express elephant

110

rifle, and plenty of ammunition for each. They had the sub-machine gun with fifty rounds left in the magazine and they each carried a pistol. And it didn't amount to a thing, considering what they had to go up against.

"I wish," Kruger was saying as he slid the bolt from the Mannlicher, "that it was only a rogue elephant."

But it wasn't. It was a dozen well-armed SS men, a company of German soldiers, their mortars, high explosives, hand grenades, and motorized equipment. It just wasn't going to be enough. They had to have the Bamilekes, and to recruit them they needed Mesotho, who was in the prison camp near the gold mine—if he was still alive.

"Tonight, I suppose," Kruger said with resignation.

"Yes."

"Any idea how we're going to pull this off, Eric? They have searchlights and machine guns, lots of barbed wire. And you can bet they'll have Mesotho in the least accessible place, well guarded."

"No," O'Reilley said, peering down the bore of the Weatherby, "I haven't got an idea in the world."

"And it's too late for Mbandaka."

"Too late for a lot of things, Paul."

"Tonight then," Kruger said with resignation. From the other room, Tami cried out in pain.

10

OLBRICHT WAS FURIOUS. His face was crimson with anger, but he held it in. Lord Gore was gone. Henshaw and his daughter were gone. This O'Reilley had gunned down two SS men and fled. His girlfriend, even after intense interrogation, could not tell them where he was, only that he had kept dozens of M-1 rifles in her room at this cabaret.

"They have it," Olbricht said once, and Hofacker turned his head to look at the SD colonel. The open car they rode in rolled through the streets of Douala. SS patrols roamed everywhere.

"You said something, sir?"

"No," Olbricht answered. "I said nothing."

But Olbricht was lying. Hofacker could see that; he could see it as easily as he could recognize the anguish, the fear on Olbricht's face. Why should there be fear there unless something had gone wrong, had gone very wrong for the Nazis?

Hofacker turned his face away. He had never belonged in a uniform, and each day it became more difficult. It was hard enough to be on the winning side, as safe as he was here, far from the raging battles. To be on the losing side, to know that there was an armed enemy closing in, was intolerable. He wondered if there were any way at all to make a run for it, taking with him a good portion of the gold the African prisoners had mined.

"What is that?" Olbricht asked abruptly as the car drove along the quay toward the submarine mooring.

Hofacker looked up and saw the streaked-gray bulk of the river patrol boat.

"Brieux's gunboat. It's been broken down since I arrived."

"It could be useful."

"No one has been able to repair it, sir."

"Or tried," Olbricht mused. "What about von Roenne's crew? They surely have equipment, and I've heard him brag about Johst, that chief engineer of his."

"I don't see what use it can be," Hofacker said weakly. Except to run him and his gold to an open port, he thought with sudden inspiration.

"You don't? You know how difficult it is to run between your camp and the city. If anyone means to attack us at Douala or at your post, he'll have to come within range of—stop, driver!—those guns. What are they? Four-inchers?" Olbricht was staring back at the gunboat, which had never seen any action. The French had brought it here twenty-three years ago for no clear purpose, and it had snapped a propeller shaft three months after that. Brieux had never tried very hard to repair it. He had no trained sailors in his company and couldn't visualize himself cruising aimlessly up and down the Sanaga River when he could be comfortably ensconced in his offices, close to the Victoria Hotel, the Equatorial Sun Bar, and the shops.

"Drive on," Olbricht ordered. The car started forward, both officers busy with their thoughts.

Hofacker wondered about the range of the gunboat. He would have to inquire. If only Olbricht weren't in the Cameroons. . . . He glanced thoughtfully that way, half-smiled, and began to mentally count the gold ingots he had stacked in the tiny shack beyond the abandoned mill.

The sun was descending. O'Reilley stood on the sagging porch of the Dutchman's house and watched as it flared out across the low clouds, flattened and dulled.

"Beautiful, isn't it?" said a voice at his shoulder, and O'Reilley turned to find Ellen Henshaw, both hands braced against the weathered porch rail. She was looking not at him but at the sunset. "I understand you're leaving tonight."

"We are, with a little luck, but we'll be back in the morning."

"A little luck?"

"A lot then," he grinned, and she smiled in response. "But we'll be back."

"Why are you doing this, O'Reilley? You were going to before you even knew about the concentration-camp reports. Is it for Mesotho? Is he that great a friend?"

"Mesotho?" O'Reilley considered. "Not really. I expect he'd kill me if there was a reason. Maybe it's just the American in me. I can't see people living enslaved. Like them or not. That goes for Africans, Jews, Belgians, and Indians."

"An idealist!" she said lightly as she turned toward him. The breeze across the veldt toyed with her curls. He studied her smile, for the first time seeing no mockery there.

"What's changed?" he asked abruptly, more throatily than he had expected.

"I don't . . . between us?"

"Yes."

"I couldn't put a name to it, O'Reilley. I'm not even sure if I was seeing you more clearly before or now. You're rough-edged and your morals are blurred. So is your personality. I thought you were an arrogant bushman who only wanted to bed me." She laughed. "That's how I see you now too, but something *has* changed. I don't know what. . . ." Her eyes were searching O'Reilley's face as he moved closer to her in the fading red light, slipped his hands around her waist, and waited. Slowly, she leaned toward him, stretching out so that her hesitant lips met his, parted and softened. "You," she said, looking not at the eyes but at the top button of his dark blue shirt where she rested one finger, "you come back, O'Reilley, or else I'll never know."

"Eric?" Paul Kruger had appeared. "It's time."

"Yes." He hesitated. He wanted to kiss her again, to say something, but he realized he had no idea what. Her arms fell away and her hand took his. They walked together into the house, where Frau Diels, apparently still sedated, sat in one corner, rocking. Doctor Henshaw's eyebrows lifted slightly as O'Reilley and his daughter came in together. Gore, holding a rifle, the .303 carbine, was a strange mixture of confidence and fear.

Paul took it upon himself to do the talking.

"We're going to take the truck part of the way. We may need it to carry Mesotho to his village. If we can get there. Lord Gore, you have the rifle." Gore nodded. "I don't know what good it will do you if the Germans come, but it may be necessary. You might have native prowlers, perhaps even a leopard—I saw some big tracks around the side of the house.

"Your best security lies in keeping your eyes open, watching the veldt. They can't penetrate the jungle behind you, and you'll see any vehicles approaching by day or night. There's three of you to stand watch in shifts, and an upstairs window just made for that.

"If they do come, and I doubt they will—no one seems to remember this house is here—you'll have time to get into the bush. After that you can make your way toward the Sanaga. They haven't got any way to get upriver, and if you have to, you can take shelter in the honeycomb caves below the falls. Hopefully, none of that will come to pass. Eric and I are going out. With luck we'll be back by sunrise. Good luck."

"Good luck to you, men," Lord Gore said with feeling.

"The box," Eric reminded everyone.

"Yes, the steel box has to be hidden. There are six of us here, and hopefully all of us will survive this war. But one of us certainly should, and the documents have to be preserved. Otherwise none of it was worthwhile. I want to live to see them all hanged, all these butchers we've seen mentioned in those papers. Especially this man." He showed them the signature on the document August Diels had sent his father in the last mail bag. "This one must not be able to deny that he and he alone was responsible for the massacre. Behind the house there's an outcropping of yellow granite. From down here you can't see it, but there's a cleft in the rock fifty feet up or so, below the shelf. From there you can just reach down to the bottom of the split, and that's where the box is, covered with jungle litter."

"Perhaps we should carry it with us," Dr. Henshaw said.

"Eric and I think there's more chance of losing it that way than in hiding it. So we'll leave it at that. Anything else, Eric?"

O'Reilley shook his head and picked up the submachine gun, slinging it over his shoulder. He wore his pistol in a flapped holster now, had a knife at his hip and the big .378 Weatherby rifle, scoped, in his other hand. He looked grim.

"How's the boy?" Kruger asked.

"Better. Still concussed, with three fractured ribs, I think. The head wound is terrible, but I've stitched it up. And I've finally been able to lance those damned boils!"

"All right then," O'Reilley said. "Let's have at it, Paul."

He looked again at Ellen, but he could bring himself to say nothing except to remind her to keep the house dark and to stay inside. Then he stumped out the back way, Kruger at his heels.

The truck rumbled across the empty plains, O'Reilley driving and Kruger, his gun muzzle out the window, staring blankly ahead. Two miles from the gold-mine camp, O'Reilley swung from the road and geared down to ease the truck into the thick mahogany-and-oil-palm forest. He turned off the ignition, cut the lights, and lit a cigarette. They sat in the silent darkness, not speaking until O'Reilley had finished smoking.

"Better wait another hour," Eric said at last.

"Think he's alive?"

"I don't know. That's the hell of it."

Everything depended on Mesotho being alive, on getting him out of there. There was an army in the jungle to the east, armed and ready, but they needed a general.

They rolled up the windows against the plague of mosquitoes and sat waiting. O'Reilley's thoughts kept drifting to Ellen. He had a strong tactile memory of her kiss, of the gentle weight of her hands. She had said she didn't know him, didn't know who he was or what he wanted. O'Reilley realized that he didn't know himself. He had come to Africa all those years ago not to escape but to explore. The years had turned into more than

116

a decade, into an inexplicable concealment, an escape from—what? From himself? Had he lost the real Eric O'Reilley in the bush years ago, deserted him along some rugged wadi? He breathed in deep to clear his head. This wasn't a time for introspection.

"Ready?" he asked. Paul nodded in the darkness, and they slipped from the truck, closing the doors quietly before trekking through the jungle and up toward the ridge that overlooked the mine. Kruger kept looking toward the horizon, both needing and fearing the arrival of the moon.

They were drenched with sweat when they threw themselves, chests heaving, against the ground at the top of the ridge. Screened partially by a brushy tangle, they could see down into the camp below. It wasn't a particularly encouraging sight.

Three watchtowers overlooked the barbed-wire triangle. Half a dozen rough shacks, each thirty feet long, housed the workers. The Sanaga River, flowing wide and placid, fronted the compound, forming the base of the triangle. The jungle growth had been cleared back to a distance of a hundred feet and low wire barriers constructed. Behind the camp, however, where O'Reilley and Kruger now lay, there was a rocky, elbow-shaped hummock some fifty feet high at the top, which had prevented the Germans from clearing the ground completely, and which would afford some sort of cover.

"No dogs," Kruger said with relief. They had heard there were dogs, but either they were kenneled, had died, or had never existed.

"They could be held in just now. Maybe they'll be let out after eating." O'Reilley said it aloud but to himself. There was no answer Kruger could make. Dogs or none, he was going down.

The schedule they had decided on was tight. O'Reilley had something less than an hour to get down, find Mesotho, and get him out before the moon rose.

Paul was fitting his scope onto his rifle. He sighted through it and said, "Not much help I can be, Eric. Not until they're breathing down our neck."

"I've got faith in you." Eric slapped him lightly on the shoulder and set his own rifle aside.

"Now?"

"I'd better go before I have too much time to think about it." They had watched the guards' routines long enough, studied the barracks, the headquarters, and the unidentifiable outbuildings—but they'd learned nothing. It was madness, O'Reilley thought, yet still he was going down.

"Luck," Paul said in a quiet, unsteady voice. Eric nodded and then slipped over the rim of the ledge, riding his haunches down to the shelf below. From there he circled eastward toward the river, and in another five minutes he was on the hummock itself, moving toward the camp. The spotlights that swept the yard and the fence line seemed much brighter now, nearer. And behind the lights were machine guns.

Eric glanced back over his shoulder, barely able to make out the bluff, let alone see Kruger. He lay on his back and rubbed dark, loamy soil over his face. Then, pistol in hand, he bellied forward—and back immediately, for twenty feet below him a German soldier in desert fatigues was walking his round. From above, they hadn't seen the sentry. In the crook of the hummock he was hidden from view. Now O'Reilley had a problem. To reach the fence line, he had to get past this man—that, or abandon the plan and circle toward the river gate, hoping some other entry would present itself.

He hung onto the lip of the rise for a minute, watching the man below him, glancing toward the camp where a clangor like that of a smith working an anvil sounded twice and ceased.

O'Reilley holstered his pistol and drew his knife from its belt sheath. Still he watched the guard. At the farthest point of his northward route, he vanished momentarily around a knobby outcropping. Each time it was ten seconds before he reemerged. O'Reilley braced himself and waited, and when the guard walked out of sight, he dropped down to a lower shelf of stone and immediately went flat. Now he was near enough to reach out and tap the guard on his shoulder when he walked past.

The soldier, glancing toward the stars, felt the sudden force of an arm clamping around his neck, felt a body collide with his own. Then he felt no more. O'Reilley's belt knife slashed across his throat, and he lay beneath the American, strangling on his own blood. O'Reilley had his hand across the German's mouth to keep him from crying out, but in another minute it was no longer necessary.

Getting to his feet, O'Reilley hooked the guard under his arms and dragged him into the thicket of monkey bush behind the rocks. As he stood over the dead man, the thought occurred to O'Reilley that this was a gift. He began stripping off his clothes, and in five minutes he was dressed in desert fatigues, carrying an automatic weapon, pacing the trail as he looked toward the compound, measuring the alertness and the numbers of its defenders. Both, he decided, were weak.

He tried to recall any German phrases he might know, then discarded the idea. His accent would probably give him away instantly.

Taking a deep slow breath, he decided to brazen it out.

There was a small gate with a kiosk standing beside it on the near side of the compound, but there seemed to be no one stationed there. He decided to simply walk in. Maybe that alone would be enough to get him shot, but he had to risk it.

Amazingly, no one called out. Perhaps it was the uniform, or the years of fighting a nonwar, but no one challenged him as he unhooked the gate in the wire and entered the prison yard.

He didn't want to hesitate now. Although he had no idea where he was going, he walked quickly as if he did. He nearly bumped into the lieutenant coming around the corner of the barracks.

O'Reilley saluted sharply and went on, not wanting to glance back. He could feel chills moving up his spine as he waited for the officer's voice to call out, or for a bullet to impact; but it had been dark and the officer had other things on his mind.

It was Lieutenant Neurath, Captain Hofacker's aide, with whom O'Reilley had nearly collided. Reluctantly, Hofacker had taken him into his confidence, knowing that he couldn't manage alone.

Neurath stopped and looked up toward the old mill where his future lay. Hundreds of thousands of marks in gold ingots. Half of it was his. Hofacker conceded that Neurath's part of this job was the most difficult but justified it by maintaining that without Hofacker Neurath would have nothing when he returned to a ravaged Germany.

And so, as O'Reilley walked across the compound, Neurath stood beneath the stars, smoking, dreaming—and planning how best to kill Colonel Georg Olbricht of the SD.

O'Reilley stopped dead in his tracks. The moan was a pitiful animal sound that was suddenly muffled. He glanced to the left and saw the camp *lazarett*, the infirmary, well lighted behind screened windows. The cry came again, and it turned Eric's stomach. They had him in the hospital. True, it didn't have to be Mesotho, but then even the Nazis didn't take people needed for labor and torture them. It had to be someone special.

The flashlight hit O'Reilley in the eyes and the big sergeant, his other hand wrapped around a pistol, shouted out, "*Was geht's Ihnen?*"

O'Reilley felt his mouth go dry, and his hand wavered between the trigger of the machine gun he carried and his belt knife. The German sergeant came nearer, holding the flashlight beam on O'Reilley's face.

Eric doubled up, clutching his belly, realizing as his hands touched his shirt fabric that the dead guard's blood had spilled down the front of it.

"*Was hat passieren? Ach! Blut!*" He shone the light on Eric's bloody hands, which were still clutching his belly. The Sergeant's voice became nearly fatherly. "*Mach dir keine Sorgen.*" He slipped his arm around Eric. "*Kommen Sie mit im Krankenhaus.*"

Taking Eric's weight, he began to lead him toward the door of the hospital. It was both good luck and bad. The sergeant wouldn't accept O'Reilley's silence for long—he would want an explanation.

120

The soldier helped Eric up the steps, and, finding the door locked, bellowed "*Hier, offen den Tür!*" He patted Eric's shoulder as they waited, and O'Reilley already regretted what he was going to have to do. The door swung open and a white uniformed orderly with a sunken, long face stood there. He said something to the sergeant, who ignored him, pushing the man aside as he brought Eric into the dispensary. The door closed behind them and Eric moved.

He brought the stock of the submachine gun up solidly beneath the sergeant's heavy jaw and the big man staggered back, going down against the wall, blood flowing from between cracked teeth. The orderly started to run, then halted, backing away as O'Reilley advanced, the muzzle of his weapon trained on the hospital man's navel.

"What is it?" he stammered in German.

"Mesotho," O'Reilley said coldly. The orderly's eyes shuttled toward a closed door across the room. O'Reilley noticed that the hands now hoisted high were fitted with rubber gloves, blood-stained.

"You're English!"

"Is he in there?" O'Reilley asked. "Come on, let's have a look."

"Dr. Schaub is in there!" the orderly squeaked. He spoke now in English that was nearly fluent. "He is conducting an experiment . . . an operation," he amended too late. O'Reilley's hand shot out and gripped the orderly by the shirt front. He hurled him toward the door, where he stopped, panting, gaping at the bloody man before him, at the tight mouth, the narrowed eyes, at the competent-looking hands holding a submachine gun.

"Open it," Eric said, his eyes flicking to the door behind him, his ears alert for any sound of someone approaching. "Now," he said, and the orderly held up a hand as if to fend off a blow.

"All right. Yes! Please don't shoot me. I'm only a medical orderly—"

"Open it."

His hand turned the knob and the door swung open into a coldly white room. O'Reilley could see the black feet protruding from the bottom of a sheet, the leather straps around the ankles.

"For God's sake, Heinz, what are you doing?" an irritable, older voice asked. He stepped nearer to the doorway, bloody scalpel in hand. He was a middle-aged man, stout and wrinkled. O'Reilley shoved on into the room and viciously backhanded the doctor, who fell with a thud and skidded against the baseboard of the wall. A quick glance at the operating table revealed two things. It was Methoso.

And it might not be for much longer.

"If you make a sound, I'll kill you," O'Reilley said to the camp doctor. "You do understand that?"

Cowering, the man nodded. His glasses hung from one ear. Blood ran from the corner of his mouth, from his nostrils. In the other room the sergeant moaned. O'Reilley said to the orderly, "Drag the soldier in here."

"Yes." He practically sprinted past O'Reilley, who followed him with his eyes. In a minute the orderly, laboring, dragged the bulky NCO into the room.

"Get some tape. Tape the sergeant up. Hands and feet— and over the mouth. Use plenty of tape. Then do the same for the doctor."

"Yes." Nervously, the orderly dug a huge roll of inch-wide adhesive tape from a cluttered drawer and got to work.

O'Reilley moved toward the operating table, and the bile rose in his throat as he saw what they had been doing to Mesotho. The cuts were all superficial—so far—but they had sliced him nearly fifty times, chest, arms, face, working their way down.

"Mesotho!" O'Reilley hissed. The dark eyes flickered open, stared out uncomprehendingly at O'Reilley for a moment before they filled with excitement. "Take it easy. Don't try to do anything on your own. We're getting the hell out of here."

The sergeant, O'Reilley saw, was gagged and bound as well as Eric would have done it himself. Heinz was doing his nervous best to please, hoping that he might stay alive. Maybe he would. The doctor struggled as Heinz approached him and began applying tape to his ankles.

"Sit still and take it!" O'Reilley said sharply. "Heinz, tell him that it's either that or I give a scalpel to Mesotho when I turn him loose."

Heinz translated in a low voice, and the doctor went ashen, his eyes goggling out of his head. He submitted to the tape job almost eagerly.

O'Reilley released Mesotho's feet and then his hands. He was naked beneath the sheet, but O'Reilley found a spare pair of white surgeon's pants and helped the African put them on while Heinz stood motionless in the corner and the doctor watched with those bulging, frightened eyes.

"I will kill him very slow," Mesotho said. His head was hanging, but his yellow eyes were alive, fixed on the doctor.

"Not now. We've got to start on out of here."

"I do not know . . ." Mesotho tried to get to his feet and couldn't make it. He slid to the floor and lay there, his blood staining the green asphalt tiles.

"You." O'Reilley returned his attention to Heinz, who hadn't moved. He looked as if he expected to die any minute, and he was damn close to it. "Is there a car around, an ambulance?"

"No. No, sir. Only the wagon."

"What wagon?"

"It is an old truck. Barely runs. We only use it . . . for the dead, sir. We take them to the cemetery by the river."

"We can't use that, not in the middle of the night."

"But that is when we take the corpses out, sir," Heinz said through dry lips. The doctor was clawing at him with his pop eyes. "You see, sir, the commandant doesn't wish the other laborers to see the wagon go out, so we do it at night when they are locked in their barracks."

"You think we could get out that way?"

"Oh, certainly. I am sure of it, sir. If I drive."

He was a little too helpful suddenly, or maybe just frightened into compliance—O'Reilley didn't know which—but there didn't seem to be any choice other than to use the old truck. If Heinz *was* telling the truth, the luck was continuing to run O'Reilley's way.

"If you're lying, you know you'll die."

"Yes, sir, I know this," Heinz managed to croak.

"All right, where is the truck?"

"In the back. There will be no trouble, sir. I usually have a helper with me. That can be you, sir. The African we can put in the back with the others."

"The others?"

"Sir." Heinz looked at his shoes. "The wagon is full."

"No, no." The voice was low, pleading.

It was Mesotho who spoke. He was a brave man, but now his eyes were filled with terror. He was superstitious. You didn't tempt the spirits by crawling in with a load of dead men.

"I cannot do it, O'Reilley."

"You have to, damn it!"

"No."

"You'll die if you stay here."

"No."

O'Reilley was beside himself with frustration. He wouldn't have relished the ride himself, but if it was between riding with the corpses and joining them, his choice would have been easy.

"I could sedate him," Heinz said.

"No." Then O'Reilley would end up carrying the injured man—something he couldn't do, although it was going to be slow enough with Mesotho as he was.

O'Reilley didn't know how to reach the old chief. He said the only thing he thought would help: "Mesotho, your people are waiting for you. If you don't go to them, if we don't stop the Germans, they'll all be in camps like this, and one by one they will all take the ride in the wagon of the dead. They need you."

"All right," Mesotho finally said. "All right, all right, all right, all right—but if my soul is gone when you see me next, O'Reilley, you will know that it is because the *tanjas* saw me among the dead and took it!" He paused. "I hurt, O'Reilley. Very badly."

"Have any painkiller?" O'Reilley asked Heinz.

"No!" Mesotho, with a supreme effort, rose to his feet. Blood ran in rivulets from the dozens of wounds, staining him red before it pooled on the floor. "I will not have these men touch me. Not again!"

"All right. Settle down." O'Reilley had his shoulder under Mesotho's arm now, propping him up. He gestured with the machine gun. "Let's go, Heinz. Stay in front of me, move very slow, and you may yet see the sun come up tomorrow."

"I understand, sir. Please." He beckoned and started moving out of the room, very slowly. The sergeant was awake now, peering dully at O'Reilley, who shrugged apologetically before he followed Heinz out, Mesotho's bloody weight against him.

"I must open the door now. I will look out and see if anyone is around," Heinz said.

"All right. Go ahead."

The orderly slid the latch and peered out into the dark yard. No moon yet.

"I see no one."

They went out, O'Reilley's eyes darting from point to point, but he saw no one. With Heinz, he helped Mesotho into the back of the rickety truck. There were six corpses lying there. One man's eyes were open, shining in the starlight. He seemed to be staring at them. Mesotho moaned deep in his throat and crawled in on hands and knees, shuddering.

It was heartless, but necessary. O'Reilley clambered up and dragged a body over, rolling it on top of Mesotho, who lay absolutely still, rigid, glaring at O'Reilley with eyes that revealed the deep loathing and fear inside him.

He'll never forgive me for this, O'Reilley thought.

He hopped down, nudged Heinz around to the passenger side, and ordered him up. "Scoot over." Then O'Reilley got in beside him, placing the machine gun on the floorboard and drawing his Beretta, which he showed meaningfully to Heinz before he lowered it again, holding it concealed beside his leg.

The truck belched to life and lurched forward, creaking and swaying toward the main gate. Searchlights still swept the yard, helmeted guards walked the perimeter. O'Reilley saw two with dogs. Heinz was stiff and pale, as if he were one of the dead.

"Relax now. Nothing's going to go wrong," O'Reilley said, and the orderly did seem to relax a little. "Carefully, calmly. Nothing to worry about."

But O'Reilley was worried. Ahead of them the main gate loomed. Two armed guards stood there, staring bleakly at the truck.

"Do they look in the back?"

"Yes, of course, but—"

"All right. Can I get out?"

"Sometimes my helper does it. Usually they don't want to."

"I'll risk it then. You keep the truck running unless they order you to shut it off. If you hear a shot, jam it into gear and get rolling. I'll be in the back."

"Yes," Heinz said distantly.

"You understand?"

"Yes."

Then maybe—if Mesotho had stopped his groaning, if they didn't see him move, if they didn't realize O'Reilley was an impostor, if Heinz didn't lose his nerve . . .

The guards stepped in front of the truck, halting it. Without saying a word, the two of them walked around to the back. O'Reilley stepped out, not wanting to risk their killing Mesotho if his respiration was detected, if a limb twitched as he lay there packed between his dead tribesmen. Maybe, O'Reilley thought gloomily, that wouldn't happen because maybe Mesotho *had* expired, a victim of his wounds and of his superstition.

The soldiers looked intensely bored. This can't have been the way they visualized spending the war. One man suddenly jumped back and shouted. O'Reilley's heart thudded heavily against his sternum, like a hammer striking there, then subsided to a wildly racing pace as he tried to translate what the guards were saying. His hand rested on his holstered Mauser pistol, the one belonging to yet another dead man who lay in the monkey bush on the hill behind the camp.

"Alive," he heard. "I tell you so."

"Yes?" The other guard peered in. He had a knife in his hand, and he struck down with it harshly as O'Reilley's hand started up with the pistol. The guard suddenly laughed.

"Yes, he's dead."

O'Reilley edged up nearer, peering into the bed of the truck, seeing the dead men stacked like cordwood. *It wasn't Mesotho!* It was the man beside him, the one with the wide-open eyes. The guard laughed again. "It was only the starlight. You're getting jumpy, Schroeder!"

O'Reilley was walking swiftly toward the cab. He was in, slamming the door, when the first guard, still laughing, waved them ahead. Heinz was sweating profusely and killed the truck when he popped the clutch. He ground the starter as the guards swung the gates open. The soldiers stood frowning, then strode slowly back toward the truck, but finally it caught. Heinz, waving to the guards, started it forward, and the death wagon rolled free of the camp as the gates swung shut behind them.

"Which way's the graveyard?"

"Left along the river."

Good. That led them back toward the hummock and concealment, possibly to freedom. There was a pale sheen to the eastern skies now. The moon was on the rise.

The old truck rattled and moaned as if the spirits of the dead it carried cried out against the night. The Sanaga was broad and dark, flowing to the sea. Upriver, far away, was the honeycomb cave where Gore, Frau Diels, and the Henshaws would take cover if the house was discovered. Hopefully they would never see the cave.

"Here we are." The truck ground to a stop and O'Reilley looked around. They were only a hundred yards or so from the camp. It was still a very tight situation. If someone decided to go into the hospital, they were done. The area had been cleared of trees and O'Reilley saw what had replaced jungle.

There was a long open trench some eighty or ninety feet

long, thirty wide, fifteen deep, and in it were scores of the dead covered with quicklime, still unburied. He looked at Heinz, his jaw clenched. The German saw something in his eyes that filled him with fear. He cowered back against the door of the truck.

"A *graveyard*," O'Reilley said. "A graveyard?"

"Work in the mines is very difficult, sir." O'Reilley's hand with the gun in it rose and Heinz covered his face. "I have nothing to do with this! I'm only an orderly, a driver, a laborer. Before the war I worked for a cobbler in Bremen! I wanted to do something more. I wanted to be in medicine and help the injured. I never knew . . ." He broke down into a fit of sobbing and O'Reilley slowly lowered his arm. Picking the machine gun up from the floorboard, he jumped out of the truck and went to the tailgate. He climbed in and began throwing the dead aside. For a terrible moment he couldn't find Mesotho. Everyone in the truck seemed to be dead.

Finally he heard the groan, and he lifted the Bamileke chief to a sitting position.

"Can you go on?"

"Do I not have to?" He looked around him. "I cannot stay here."

"You'll do." O'Reilley grinned in the darkness. "Come on, we've got a lot of work to do."

"Yes." There was something somber and mad in Mesotho's voice that chilled O'Reilley. He shook it off and helped Mesotho from the truck. The moon was a golden glow now above the hills. Mesotho, leaning against O'Reilley, stood gaping at the pit before him.

"Closer," he said. They could hear Heinz still sobbing in the truck. Nothing else sounded but the Sanaga rumbling past. They eased toward the long trench, and Mesotho stood staring at the dead who were tangled together, white with the lime, ghostly and revolting.

"So," he said. "The Germans."

"We've got to get out of here," O'Reilley said.

"Yes."

"And make a war against these people, Mesotho."

"Yes. I know that man there." A black finger spotted with dried blood poked out. "Look here, that is M'baga. And there. His son."

"We've got to go, Mesotho."

"Yes," he said heavily. "But I wish you would have let me kill the doctor-German."

There wasn't time to tie and gag Heinz, and O'Reilley couldn't bring himself to kill him. He believed his story, that he was only a confused, betrayed young man. Maybe he was wrong— the tears could have been for his own death—but O'Reilley preferred to err on the side of life.

The orderly didn't cry out or beep the horn or run back toward the compound as O'Reilley, bearing most of Mesotho's weight, moved off jerkily toward the elbow-shaped hummock ahead of them.

They had to swing wide. Mesotho couldn't climb. O'Reilley had some confidence now. With the moonlight, Kruger could see enough to cover their retreat if anyone decided to pursue. For the moment no one did. All they had to do was make it past the old mill and reach the canyon that ran up to the plateau where Kruger and the truck waited. Then they'd head back to the Dutchman's house after a stop at Mesotho's village to organize his people, to issue the rifles and send them into the jungle to hunt.

It didn't seem like much. The worst part was over. They climbed up out of the stream bed and started toward the old mill, and the guns opened up from out of the darkness.

11

O'REILLEY FLUNG HIMSELF to the dark earth and Mesotho fell with him. At first O'Reilley thought the Bamileke had been hit, but he seemed to be all right—though he might not be for long.

Like dozens of winking red eyes muzzle flashes spotted the night. The thunder of the guns chattered in O'Reilley's ears. Tracers streaked the night with deadly bands of color.

Realizing that the worst thing he could do would be to fire back and mark their position, O'Reilley held off, lying pressed to the ground, Mesotho's motionless body next to his.

It was the last place he had expected to encounter a force of this size. Perhaps a single guard, but there were easily a dozen men out there with automatic weapons. Why? There was nothing at the mill.

"Back," O'Reilley said, and he began creeping back down the wash, Mesotho dragging himself along. O'Reilley handed the African his Beretta, which Mesotho took with pleasure. How good he would be with it was uncertain; he had probably never had a handgun in his possession. But Mesotho was innately skilled with all weapons.

O'Reilley froze. Above them they could hear soldiers rushing toward their position. The bright moon behind them was like a searchlight. The first German appeared, a stark silhouette against the skyline. O'Reilley started to squeeze off but never got the chance. The soldier buckled at the knees and slumped forward, skidding down the slope on his face. A split second later came the distant, rolling report of a heavy rifle.

"One for Paul," Eric muttered. There was no mistaking the

big .458 Mannlicher. There seemed to be confusion above. A shout went up, and then the Mannlicher spoke four times in rapid succession. Another man cried out and O'Reilley held Mesotho to the ground. The bullets from Paul's rifle, propelled by its amazing force—five thousand foot-pounds—would pass cleanly through the body of a soldier with plenty of killing power to spare.

"We've got to move," O'Reilley hissed. The guns chattered away above them, but Paul was drawing most of their fire.

"Yes. This is no place to be."

Which was an understatement. Machine-gun bullets raked the trees around them, spattering bark and leaves, severing limbs from the ebony and rubber trees. How to escape was the question, how to reach the plateau? Mesotho seemed to read Eric's mind. "I can run, I can fight," the African said, and clearly he meant it.

"All right. Across the road there at Paul's next volley."

"That is Kruger up there?"

"Yes."

The Mannlicher opened up again, its deadly, deep-throated boom somehow more ominous than the rattling staccato of the German machine guns. And, knowing Paul, he was hitting something with each round.

"Now!"

Mesotho was up and hobbling forward as O'Reilley laid down a barrage of submachine-gun fire. There was little response. Kruger had pinned them, and the abruptness of Eric's counterattack seemed to keep them down.

The submachine gun suddenly clicked empty, and O'Reilley simply dropped the weapon, continuing on, scrambling up the slope beyond the mill with Mesotho wheezing and staggering behind, his wounds opening up again.

The night suddenly fell silent. There was a single, abbreviated burst of gunfire behind them and then nothing as they clambered up the moon-scoured slope.

Mesotho had halted cold, his head thrown back, trying to

fill his lungs with strength. It wasn't particularly successful. His body had suffered too much. But he managed to keep moving, and that was all that counted.

Half an hour later they scaled the last eight feet of stony bluff and rolled, exhausted, up onto the rim of the ledge where Paul Kruger, still hunkered down behind his rifle, had covered their retreat.

"Damn you, Eric!" Kruger said wildly. "I don't believe it. I don't believe you're here. I don't," he repeated, "bloody believe it!"

Neither did O'Reilley, not really. A wonderful feeling of relief washed over him.

Then his mood changed abruptly. "Let's get going, Paul. We've got a war to make and a . . . some people waiting for us."

They jog-trotted to the truck, Mesotho hanging between them. The Ford roared to life, and they were off on a swaying run toward the Bamileke village.

"Now we will show them," Mesotho said. "The guns are at the high village. My people!" Then he asked O'Reilley, "What of my son, Tami? I was told the Germans had him."

"He's safe, thanks to Paul. Dr. Henshaw is taking care of him."

"In Douala?"

"They're at the Dutchman's house."

"Good. You are a good warrior, O'Reilley. After this is over, I shall drive all the whites from this country of ours, but for now I am happy you are with us."

"And Kruger."

"And Kruger," Mesotho said, glancing only once, briefly, at the South African.

The leopard roared out again, a bone-chilling, primitive sound. A deadly thing walked the earth, looking for living meat to devour. Frau Diels shivered and then, bracing herself with a deep breath, went on. The climb was a long one. Below, the old house sat unlighted against the veldt. There was no light in all the world save the moon, but that was light enough.

These Engländers, these enemies of the Reich, had hidden the papers there, in the rocks above the house. To think that her husband had been a part of this. To think that treachery had rooted itself in her own family!

She slipped as she climbed the yellow rocks and fell back, scraping her knees and elbow. Blood flowed—that had no importance; only the paper had importance. The one paper, the paper that incriminated the Führer. As if the Führer were a convict, a savage thing like the prowling leopard!

He was a god on earth. He was the hope of the German people, of the world. If the letter could be recovered, it must be. Only then could the good name of Diels be spoken again with pride.

She was there finally, and, panting, her fingers scraping against stone, she dug the iron box from its hiding place. There were many documents in there, many. Her husband had been such a fool!

None of the rest of the papers mattered—only the one, only the one with the holy name, and with shaking hands she searched, finding the paper by the light of the moon, hiding it in her night dress, where it nestled warmly between her breasts—a paper *his* hands had touched, *his* pen had signed.

She feverishly closed the box, jammed it back into its hidden crevice, and started down the bluff, moving quickly, very quickly, so that her holy mission could be completed before the enemy, O'Reilley and his South African ally, could return.

It was a peering eye, the moon, searching the house where Ellen Henshaw sat waiting. Waiting for what she did not know. For the dawn, for Armageddon, for a waking time when all of this would be revealed as a horrid dream.

For Eric O'Reilley. Whoever he was, whatever he wanted, this cheerful, wry, copper-haired man who'd thrust himself into her life.

Count von Roenne had said the American loved her, and

seeing O'Reilley's eyes that night, she had nearly believed him. Paul Kruger, too, had said that Eric loved her. Yet O'Reilley never said it. Or perhaps he had and she hadn't been listening. Her head came around at the sound of approaching footsteps. Lord Gore came into the upstairs room, a bedroom that smelled now of animals, of dust and mold.

"You'd better get some sleep," he said. "It's my watch."

"Shouldn't they be back?" she asked out of the darkness.

"No," Gore said with transparent and touching dishonesty. "It's far too early."

Ellen rose from the window seat and gave Gore the rifle, happy that it was in his hands now, that his eyes had the responsibility of watching for the Germans.

She was weary yet doubted she could sleep. Tami would cry out with pain from time to time. A lion had roared near the barn not an hour ago. The house seemed alive with slithering things, and outside the night was filled with approaching evil.

Downstairs she could hear Frau Diels sleeping, a fluttering snore escaping her nostrils. Tami muttered unhappily in his sleep.

"How is he?" Ellen's father was standing beside the injured boy's makeshift bed, just watching. His head came around.

"I believe he'll be all right. If we had him in a hospital, I'd guarantee it. I only hope we aren't forced to move him." He slipped an arm around his daughter and kissed her forehead. "You'd better get what sleep you can, Ellen."

"Yes," she agreed, and, making a bed in the corner, she curled up to try to do just that. She never did get to sleep, reaching only some half-dreaming state where O'Reilleys with elephant tusks chased her through the bush naked.

A hand shook her shoulder and she sat up instantly. "Shh!" It was Lord Gore, his face deeply creased in the faint light that spilled through the window.

"What?" she asked in a little squeak.

"There's someone coming. I can see the lights of a vehicle."

"O'Reilley?"

"I can't tell. Just get up and be ready, please, Ellen. And waken Frau Diels. Your father is already up."

Ellen tugged on her shoes and got to her feet dizzily. She wanted to peek out through the tattered curtains but instead shook Frau Diels awake. She sat up out of a deep, drugged sleep and stared blankly at Ellen. There was a bit of spittle pooled at the corner of her mouth.

"Get up, please," Ellen whispered. "We may have to move soon."

"What is it? Who is it?" Frau Diels demanded.

"We don't know yet."

"It's the SS!"

"We don't know. Please. Get your shoes on."

"Yes, my shoes. My shoes," she gabbled. Ellen went upstairs to where Gore and Doctor Henshaw crouched, looking out across the plateau. Now Ellen, too, could see the headlights bouncing toward them, see the moonlit dust cloud streaming out behind the vehicle.

"It's a truck," Lord Gore said. "Still can't make out the type."

"My God," Henshaw breathed. "It's them. There's a swastika on the door."

"No." Lord Gore wasn't convinced, didn't want to be convinced. "You're wrong, Michael. There's no . . . damn it all to hell!" He turned, his mouth twitching. "It is. All right. Calmly. Out the back door."

"Wait," Ellen whispered sharply. "They're stopping. They're not coming up to the house."

Gore held the motheaten curtains apart with two fingers. "The water tower. Could there still be water in it? Of course, it's an open cistern. Someone's getting out." He laughed nervously. "They're only filling the radiator."

The minutes passed with painful slowness, feeble things creeping past the window as they watched the Germans fill the radiator. Two of them smoked, and Gore saw someone poke a head out from the back of the truck. Something was shouted.

Finally the hood was closed and latched shut. The Germans climbed back into the truck, and they could see a white puff of smoke as it started.

"Now, if they don't come this way—" Lord Gore muttered.

"I know they will. Damn them. Why else come all the way up here?" Henshaw said.

Ellen was gripping her father's sleeve tightly, her eyes aching from staring out the greasy, filthy window, afraid that if she blinked she would miss seeing what came next.

"They're turning!" Gore's laugh was more of a strangled groan. "They're heading toward the river!"

It was then that they heard the slam downstairs, heard the shrill cry and realized with despair what was happening. "Frau Diels!"

They could hear her calling the soldiers now. "Come here! Come here! My colonel, I have it! I have the paper!" She waved her arms frantically. The truck had stopped, and now two men jumped from the back of it. "Here! Here!" she cried, and the machine guns stuttered a response. She crumpled up, an unstrung marionette, and lay against the grass.

Ellen couldn't move, couldn't draw a breath. The two soldiers were running toward Frau Diels's body. The truck was turning, its headlight beams whitening the dry grass.

"Quickly! There's no more time," Doctor Henshaw said. He grabbed his burlap sack and rifle. Shoving Ellen before him, he made for the stairs, Lord Gore trailing right behind.

"The boy," Ellen said.

"Yes, yes, I'll get him."

The machine guns spoke again. A snowstorm of shattered glass flew across the room as the windows in the front of the house were peppered with gunfire. Bullets whined off the stone porch and chimney, buried themselves in the walls, tearing them to splinters.

"Down!" Ellen felt a hand yank her to the floor. Then she was crawling across the glass-littered floor toward the back of the house. Her hands and knees were cut, warm with blood. They heard the truck roar into the yard.

136

"Go on, Ellen, we've got Tami," her father called, and she chanced rising to a half-crouch, running toward the back door. If they could get to the bush, if they could get a minute's lead. . . . Her father and Lord Gore appeared, Tami slung between them.

She held the door for them as they raced through, rapping the boy's head on the frame. The machine gun opened up again and Ellen thought she screamed. She couldn't be sure of anything with the noise, the hail of bullets. It was dark in the backyard, despite the moon. Gore and Henshaw were running toward the jungle-covered bluff, Henshaw looking back frantically for Ellen, who had stopped to recover their food and her father's bag. They would need those to survive.

She started forward again and heard with anguish the shout to her right, saw the twin beams of light rounding the corner of the house. She hesitated and then had no choice. She couldn't cross the clearing. She began to run, ducking behind the barn, hearing the whine of the truck engine, the loud shouts, the occasional burst of gunfire.

She tripped, went down, and scrambled to her feet again, making for the brush-clotted ravine beyond the barn. She could see now that she wasn't going to reach it. The truck skirted the barn and roared after her. She looked around frantically, and seeing the shallow depression, an old animal wallow, she rolled into it and lay there, her heart hammering wildly as the Germans raced toward her.

The headlights blinked across her. Two men with automatic weapons were to her right. There was a lot of noise from the house as doors were bashed in.

Ellen pressed her face to the earth, feeling the bristle of stubbled grass against her cheek. She could hear them shouting all around her.

They should have known, she thought, should have known that Frau Diels was unreliable. Probably she was a stout Nazi. Or perhaps deranged. She had withered and stiffened after her husband had been relieved of duty. Maybe she had hoped to redeem the family name—who knew?—it didn't matter now.

She only hoped her father and Lord Gore had made it. And that somewhere on this night Eric O'Reilley was alive. She thought of him now with unexpectedly strong feelings, remembering his grin, the shy gruffness of him, the large hands covered by hair like brass wire.

She realized that it was quieter. Her eyebrows drew together in puzzlement. Then she realized that the truck had turned away. They hadn't seen her!

She lifted her eyes, peering out of the depression. There were soldiers around the house and near the barn. There was no chance at all of making it to the bluff where her father had gone with Gore and Tami.

Then where? She couldn't remain. If sunrise found the Germans still here, she would certainly be taken prisoner. And she wasn't strong enough—no one was—to avoid telling them everything they wanted to know.

No, she had to move. Her mind reluctantly came to grips with the problem. Go where? She was cut off from following the men. Go where? And how?

Looking cautiously around, she saw the dark line of brush that marked the edge of the ravine. Now it was possible to make it there. And once she had gotten that far? Home—it was the only alternative that occurred to her. To somehow walk the distance back to Douala, take refuge with someone. Perhaps they didn't even know she was involved—perhaps she could simply wait things out there. That seemed remote, but she had no idea what else to do.

"One step at a time, girl," she told herself sternly. Looking again toward the house, she crawled out of the far side of the wallow, moving on bloody hands and knees toward the ravine. It was an endless trek, painful as the glass dug in deeper, but eventually she made it without being seen.

Ellen practically flung herself down into the ravine, feeling the brush tear at her flesh. She had escaped! She didn't pause for breath but pushed on rapidly toward Douala, not knowing what she would do once she got there, not knowing with any certainty if she or her loved ones would live to see the sun come up over the dark continent.

"There. Again." Paul Kruger stopped the Ford truck and leaned his head out the window. "Hear it, Eric? Shots, and plenty of them. Maybe the Dutchman's place."

"We knew it might happen," he answered, forcing himself to be calm. "The contingency plan was well laid out. They'll simply move through the bush toward the cave."

"Then why all the shooting?" Kruger mused. Gore and Henshaw wouldn't have stood their ground. They knew they would have no chance.

"I think they like their guns," Mesotho said, and maybe he was right. Eric O'Reilley tried to make himself believe this.

"Let's get moving, Paul!" O'Reilley snapped. "We're not doing anybody any good sitting here." The truck started forward again.

Mesotho muttered to himself for a bit. When he had stopped, he explained. "I asked the *tanjas* to look away when my son Tami walks past their death holes." He added offhandedly, "Also I spoke for the white people."

"How far to the village?"

"You know the high village, O'Reilley," Mesotho said in surprise. Then he realized that Eric didn't want to talk about Tami and the white people. "One mile. Then I can be healed. My wives will put medicine on me. Then"—his voice lowered to a rumbling bass—"we will show the Germans that our guns can also make much noise."

A few minutes later they were rattling through the high village. It was upriver from the newer camp, which the Germans had destroyed. It was practically on the Sanaga River, half a mile below the nameless falls that tumbled down over the slate-gray stone shelf, creating a short stretch of rapids. Their roar was like distant thunder.

They heard the falls only briefly, for as the Bamilekes realized that the truck brought their war leader, they poured into the village from the jungle, their shouts and screams filled the air, their dancing bodies crushing together as they pressed nearer Mesotho, chanting his name. Despite his severe injuries, Mesotho managed to stand upright and walk through them toward his hut. O'Reilley and Kruger followed behind him.

Two calm young women, one wearing a woven shawl, the other naked except for a cotton skirt knotted at her waist, stood awaiting Mesotho, as if they had expected his return that evening. Outside, the noise and the dancing continued. O'Reilley and Kruger entered the Bamileke hut. The women started clucking as they got a good look at Mesotho's wounds. Mesotho lowered himself heavily onto a red-and-black woven mat and stretched out.

"Tomorrow there will be no gold-mine camp to do this to people," Mesotho said. "I swear it."

A man stuck his head in the door and Mesotho shouted out a spate of Bantu. The man ducked away. "I have sent them for the guns."

"Mesotho, don't try to take those machine guns on."

"I have said the camp will be no more tomorrow."

One of his wives was crouched down, painting his wounds with something gooey and white, her dark, handsome face reflecting deep concern.

"All right," O'Reilley said, squatting down. "I understand that, but it does no one any good if you just charge on up there. You've got to snipe the men in the towers first, understand?"

"No." He winced as his wife touched a particularly bad wound.

"Let me show you." O'Reilley began to sketch a plan of attack for Mesotho, who followed each point carefully. "Paul and I—" Eric began at one point, but Mesotho interrupted.

"This battle is not your battle. You will not go!"

"Paul can pick them out of the towers easily."

"No," Mesotho answered flatly. "This is my battle. It is my people who have been murdered. O'Reilley," he said after a minute, "I want you to go to Tami. I want you to stay with him. If I win my war, bring him to me." Then, just for a moment, Mesotho's dark hand rested on O'Reilley's. It was there, and then it was withdrawn and the yellow eyes of the Bamileke were hard again. "I know you are worried about the white people anyway," he added as if to satisfy some sense of honor.

"All right, Mesotho," O'Reilley agreed. "It's your way then. But let's go over the battle plan again. Let us get your men together and make sure they understand those weapons. There's no time for target practice now; besides, the shots would bring trouble. But let's at least make sure they know how to jack a shell into the chamber and sight."

"Yes, we will do that, O'Reilley. Then you must go to Tami—and the white people. I must go and kill the others. All of them, all of those filthy things which live to worship this Iron Web. They must live no more."

12

It was the hour before dawn, when the birds began to rustle and the prowling cats moved back into the jungle and Ellen Henshaw reached Lord Gore's house. Her feet were cut to ribbons, her throat and mouth parched. She was too tired now to feel fear, too much in pain to know what she was doing or to care. She simply went to the back of the governor's mansion and, after trying a locked door, climbed in through an open window. It didn't surprise her that there were no guards—after all, what was there to protect?

She wanted a bath. Could she do that? Ellen dragged herself along the hallway. She could get bandages and antiseptic from her father's room—unless the Germans had taken them. No, a bath first. . . . She reeled and collided with the wall, straightening up again only with difficulty. A bracer, she thought; a stiff drink is what I need most.

She halted, puzzled, her bearings confused, then started toward the drawing-room sideboard where Lord Gore kept what little brandy he had left.

It was still dark inside the house, but now a little cold gray predawn light seeped through the stained dormer window. Ellen hesitated, sensing something, but she was too weary to heed it even if there had been anything to do but plod ahead.

She poured brandy from Lord Gore's decanter into a small silver-leafed crystal goblet. Then she turned, her back to the sideboard, and saw the man in uniform sitting in the high-backed leather chair, watching her.

Oddly, Ellen's reaction was not fear, but a chilly anger that caused her exhausted body to tremble. She drank down the brandy and said, "Good morning, Count von Roenne."

"Good morning," the submarine commander said, recrossing his legs.

"May I ask what you are doing here?"

"Temporary quarters. And may I ask what you are doing here, Miss Henshaw?"

"I live here."

"But one understood you were running around in the bush making revolution."

"*Did one?*" she asked venomously, pouring another drink.

"You should eat before drinking. Always."

Ellen didn't answer. She heard the chair squeak as Roenne rose, then felt his presence at her shoulder.

"Where have you been?" he asked.

"Out in the garden." She drank the brandy down. This time it stung her nostrils, lit small fires in her lungs.

Roenne was looking her over, the torn hands, the ripped skirt and blouse. "A rose garden, one assumes," he said dryly.

"All right! I am a revolutionist. Guilty!" The brandy was performing tricks in her brain. The room swirled. Or was that the exhaustion? "Now may I take a bath before you torture me?"

"Yes," Roenne said. "Please do so. But I do not mean to torture you."

"Oh, of course not." She laughed disparagingly. "You are the man of honor, the knight of Baden-Württemberg, the country gentleman!"

"Yes," Roenne said, his expression calm, "that is me. You have identified me correctly."

"And you will turn me in."

"Of course," Roenne said with a smile, "but first I will allow you a bath."

"The difference between a gentleman and a butcher," Ellen said bitterly, slamming the goblet down against the sideboard. The brandy was working.

"What is all this talk of butchery, of torture?"

"Ask the millions who have suffered it."

"The soldiers?" Roenne asked blankly.

"The civilians, the noncombatants, the subhumans, the Jews, the Bolsheviks, the Slavs. Yes, and any German who opposed this policy."

"Do I sense propaganda at work?"

"Propaganda, yes." Ellen pushed a tired hand through her auburn hair. "That's all it is. Propaganda in the Reich's official reports."

"What are you talking about?"

"You've never heard of the KZs, I suppose."

"Of course I have. But then not much is said about them. No one seems to know much."

"Ask the SS. They know plenty. Now"—she pushed past him and started for the stairway—"I am going to bathe. If you kill me afterward, then that's that. I am at least going to have a bath!" Her voice rose shrilly and von Roenne, eyes narrowing, watched her walk away. Shrugging, he poured himself a drink from the same decanter she had used. Then he settled again into his chair.

It was a full hour before Ellen appeared again, her skin pinkened, scented lightly, her hands bandaged. She had put on a yellow cotton dress that complimented her figure.

"I'm ready," she said, lifting her chin.

"Ellen, please," von Roenne said. "It is my duty to take you to Olbricht. My honor demands it."

Ellen gave a small snort of derision.

"Duty, country, honor," Roenne intoned as if saying his catechism. "But if there are extenuating circumstances—if, for example, you were drawn into this unwillingly, unknowingly—then we must try to prove it. I wish only to help you."

"Yes," she said dully. She had turned her back on the naval captain. Now she spun toward him and said, "Extenuating circumstances. Are there any in our case?"

"I don't—"

"The case against you, against Germany. The case for inhuman barbarism, which is overwhelmingly strong against you and which demands the death penalty for your nation."

"You have had too much to drink."

"Have I?" She paused, obviously debating something in her mind. "There is extenuating evidence," Ellen said quietly.

"Then let me see it," von Roenne said with relief.

"It's not here. It's . . . miles away."

"I can get a car."

"We have to go alone."

"Of course."

Still she hesitated. Was she being a fool, betraying the effort of the others? "Bring your car," she answered.

They drove in silence to the Dutchman's house, up the narrow winding road and across the plain. The sun was hot, impossibly so; it bludgeoned the land and the creatures that crawled across it. Ellen sat in a daze, her ears ringing, her throat dry. Once she glanced at von Roenne, who was driving intently, cautiously. He wants to kill me, she thought, to satisfy his honor.

"Slow down now," she said. "There were soldiers here. SS men."

But they were gone. Frau Diels's body was gone. Only the house remained, its windows blasted out, door broken and twisted. Roenne pulled around to the back and parked the car in the shade of the barn.

"Now then?"

"Come on." There was no changing her mind now. She had to trust von Roenne. She led him up onto the outcropping and, easing forward toward the edge, found the crevice. Her hand groped for the steel box, and for a moment she thought it had been taken, but finally her fingers touched smooth, painted steel and she brought it up into the harsh yellow sunlight.

"This is it?" von Roenne asked. "This explains why you were with the rebels?"

"Yes," she said, thrusting it at him, "this explains it."

He sat down then on the edge of the outcropping and lit a cigarette before opening the box. He slipped the top folder

145

from it and read the title: *Quarterly report, Commanding Officer, Auschwitz KZ.*

He flipped it open idly as Ellen sat beside him, looking across the distances toward the coolly gleaming, jewelled sea beyond Douala.

She glanced at the count from time to time, trying to read his expression, failing. He sat there for more than an hour in the broiling sun while chimpanzees, vervets, and parrots squawked and screamed in the jungle behind them. A herd of impala moved out nervously to graze.

The sun was directly overhead when he finished. Von Roenne lit another cigarette, placed the folders carefully away, and closed the lid. Ellen didn't speak until he was through smoking.

"Well?" she demanded.

"I understand your actions," he answered expressionlessly.

"That is all you have to say?"

"Yes." He rose then, dusting off his uniform. "We must get back to Douala."

"Even seeing the signature of your Führer on these papers is not enough to convince you of the evil of this dark Reich?" Ellen asked in anguish.

"I don't understand you."

"The paper—there—the one with his name signed to it."

"But, Ellen, there is no paper with the Führer's signature," said von Roenne.

"There must be!"

"No." He shuffled through the papers. "That does not matter, however. We must return to Douala."

"And you're turning me in to Olbricht, giving him the box?"

"I'm not turning you in." He handed her the box. "This is yours. Put it back where you found it."

Ellen took it, disconcerted and angry, and placed the box back in the cleft. Von Roenne was silent as he drove rapidly back to Douala.

"The best thing for you to do is to stay in the governor's house," he said as they approached the town limits. "In your old room. I will say, truthfully, that you are my prisoner if anyone should discover you."

"Count von Roenne—"

"It is best we do not speak," he said sharply, and Ellen lapsed into a helpless silence. The car rattled on and she slept. She could not help it. She felt defeated, and as von Roenne guided the car homeward, she slept.

"Yes?" Brieux said irritably. "Just a minute!" But the pounding at the door continued. The French Legion commander rose, groaning, from his habitual noonday nap. He always left orders never to be roused. He glanced at the tightly drawn curtains, seeing the line of white light that seeped onto the floor beneath them.

Brieux rolled away from the sleeping woman and pulled his robe on.

It was Sergeant Lamarck at the door, his expression bland, his eyes empty.

"What now, Lamarck?"

"Sorry, sir," the legionnaire said, saluting. "I thought this was of sufficient importance to—"

"What *is* it?" Brieux asked, rubbing his forehead in agitation.

"One of the African auxiliaries, sir. He's spotted Lord Gore and Dr. Henshaw. Upriver, moving in the direction of the falls."

Brieux looked toward the bed where Marie lay, the sheet clinging to the contour of her hip and thigh, breast and shoulder.

"All right, Sergeant, very good."

"What shall I do, sir?"

"Do? Nothing. You have made your report."

The door was closed in Lamarck's face and he stood there biting at his lower lip. Major Brieux was crazy. He knew that the Germans were frantic trying to find Gore and Henshaw.

How could he forget it and crawl back into bed with that woman? It was a good way to get oneself shot.

Lamarck walked out into the morning and hesitated only briefly before getting into his Fiat and driving back uptown toward the Victoria Hotel, where Colonel Olbricht stayed.

Ellen heard the Mercedes pull into the yard, and she looked out to see it brake to a stop before the door of the governor's house. Two SS men hopped out, and she felt her heart sink. Von Roenne had turned her in after all. And now he would triumphantly reveal the location of the steel box. He would receive yet another oak-leaf cluster to wear on that Knight's Cross of his. No doubt that would satisfy this sense of "honor" he was so pleased with.

She started for the door, opened it, and then paused. They were speaking in rapid German, but Ellen could follow most of it.

"To the wharf, Captain von Roenne. Immediately. Colonel Olbricht is waiting even now."

"To my submarine?" von Roenne asked in some surprise.

"No, sir. The gunboat. Your engineer has repaired the propeller shaft and the steering problem."

"But I fail to understand—"

"It will be explained by Colonel Olbricht. This is an order, sir."

"Yes, of course."

Ellen could see von Roenne downstairs through the crack of the open door. She saw him retrieve his hat, glance once toward her room, and then follow the SS men out of the house.

She went to the window and watched them get in, watched the car race away down the gravel driveway. Then she walked to the bed, sagged onto it and sat staring at the wall, tears of exhaustion brimming in her eyes.

Von Roenne was driven to the docks in minutes. The SS men leaped from the open Mercedes and started running toward the ancient gunboat. The count sauntered after them. He saw Colonel Olbricht standing at the rail, his face red with anger. Rudi Johst appeared, glanced at his captain, and went below.

Brieux was also there, looking chastened. Hofacker was there too, with his aide, Neurath, and the dozen remaining SS men.

"Sir." Von Roenne saluted and Olbricht glowered.

"We are going upriver in pursuit of the criminals Gore and Henshaw, Captain von Roenne. Please get us underway."

Roenne, who had never operated the forty-foot gunboat, nodded as if there were nothing unusual in Olbricht's order. He looked around, seeing Fritzche and Horst Best, Stutters and Reinhardt. They all looked confused. What the hell were they supposed to do on this tub?

"Weigh anchor," Roenne said sharply. "Lieutenant Fritzche, to the wheelhouse with me."

Fritzche spun and followed his captain. "What are we doing?" he muttered under his breath. Von Roenne didn't answer him. He climbed to the bridge and studied the controls for a minute.

"Johst!" He leaned out and waved to catch the eye of his engineer. "Are we ready?"

"Ready, sir."

"Fine. Now climb up here and show me how to start the engine."

Ten minutes later they were chugging up the Sanaga, making slow headway against the current. The SS men got behind the twin four-inch guns and, after a few minutes' discussion, fired three practice rounds into the jungle, felling ebony and bamboo, and sending a flock of white, long-winged birds skyward in a screeching cloud.

Olbricht was climbing to the bridge as von Roenne continued to adjust the choke. Behind him was a tattooed Furlani.

"This man will show you where to stop," Olbricht said. "There are supposed to be some caves on the north side of the river. The guns will bring them out of there or bury them. . . . What in the hell is that!"

A hailstorm of small-arms fire was audible somewhere in the distance. Olbricht's head jerked around frantically. He shouted down to Hofacker, "Where is that coming from?"

Hofacker, hands cupped to his lips, called back, "The camp! Ahead! My camp!"

"Greater speed, von Roenne," commanded Olbricht.

There was absolutely no way to increase speed against the current, with the engine in the shape it was, but Roenne nodded. "Yes, sir," he said, and attempted to look as if he were speeding up the boat.

The jungle lining the riverbank suddenly parted as they came around a bend, and they caught sight of the battle. The gold mine and the adjacent camp were under intense attack. The gunfire was continuous.

"To the guns!" Olbricht commanded, and his prize pet dogs, Ziegler and Erzberger, leaped to the four-inchers. The rifle fire was suddenly turned on the gunboat, and von Roenne ducked as dozens of rounds punched through the wheelhouse walls, one striking an oil line.

He veered away from the shore, but Olbricht commanded, "Go in nearer, nearer! They'll run once they hear the big guns."

The four-inchers opened up. The first shell was a dead hit on a German watchtower. Roenne saw it buckle, saw the machine-gunners cartwheel through the air to land on the ground, saw a band of black prisoners rushing toward them, chanting something incomprehensible, beating them to death. The rifle fire only increased, and Roenne crouched down to steer, moving yet nearer to the shore as the big guns belched flame and smoke, the boat swaying madly with each detonation.

"Shear off, von Roenne!" Olbricht screamed. "Shear off!"

He did so, and the boat putted on, bullets following them for a quarter of a mile before they rounded another bend in the Sanaga. Three men were dead aboard the gunboat: two SS men and a Sergeant Lamarck of the French Foreign Legion.

Olbricht, red-faced and panting, murmured over and over, "I'll deal with them. I'll show them something."

Lieutenant Neurath stood at the rail, watching the gray bow part the blue-green waters of the Sanaga. His Luger was cocked and ready. Everything was working perfectly. They had the boat repaired now. Only Olbricht stood in the way. Once things quieted down at the camp, they could bring the gold down from the old mill, load it on the gunboat, and sail off to an open port where passage could be arranged for South America. But first, Olbricht.

Neurath looked again at his commanding officer, who was pale and trembling. Hofacker was badly frightened, badly in need of alcohol, but he, too, was ready.

They anticipated no resistance. Once things were explained to the other SS men—at gunpoint if necessary—they would rise to the bait of the gold. They would gladly throw in their lots with Neurath and Hofacker. Later, some plan could be devised to eliminate them.

Olbricht was now clambering down the ladder from the wheelhouse. Neurath checked his pistol and then put it in his jacket pocket. He started toward Olbricht, Hofacker behind him.

"Colonel . . ." Neurath drew his pistol and thrust it in Olbricht's face, but the panic-stricken colonel slapped outward with his forearm, and Neurath's pistol exploded beside Olbricht's ear. Hofacker had his sidearm in his hand, but he was frozen, unable to fire it as Olbricht clung to Neurath, clawing desperately at his own holstered Luger. Olbricht was enraged. He had hold of Neurath's right sleeve at the cuff, and the lieutenant's second shot also flew wide, splintering the weathered rail behind Olbricht.

"Hofacker, fire, you fool!" Neurath shouted as he grappled with the colonel. Hofacker groaned out loud. Implicated now, he had no choice but to attempt to kill Olbricht.

The burst of the machine gun was deafening. Pain stitched across his body from hip to shoulder, and he was driven over the rail into the Sanaga, staining it briefly red before the current swallowed him.

Olbricht twisted his gun hand up and fired at point-blank range into Neurath's abdomen and the young lieutenant's head snapped forward, his mouth contorting as the bullet severed his spine. He fell to the deck and lay there, fingers twitching, before Olbricht put a second 9mm. round through his neck.

"Overboard," Olbricht said, stepping back, hatless, panting. Erzberger and Ziegler saw to it, throwing the lieutenant into the river to join his commander. Olbricht retrieved his hat and stood gasping, pistol still in hand, watching the river ahead of them. Once he glanced at von Roenne, but the naval captain was intent on his work, his handsome face disinterested, businesslike.

"Sir?" Ulrich Ziegler was there, his eyes flashing. The killing had begun. Ziegler was content. "Are you all right? What happened? What did they want?"

The gold, of course. Olbricht knew this, but he intended to keep it a secret. "Traitors to the Reich. They sold out to Gore and his friends."

That satisfied Ziegler, who had little imagination. When he did imagine, when he dreamed, it was mostly of people exploding in a cloud of blood before his gunsights.

The African had come down to the deck. He was pointing excitedly ahead, jabbering away.

"Where's Brieux? What is he saying?"

The legionnaire was summoned, and he translated. "Just ahead, he says. Just ahead are the caves. That is where Gore and his friends are."

"Have von Roenne pull in nearer the shore now." Olbricht's eyes lighted. Somewhere in the distance they could hear a waterfall rumbling. And above them was a rising, pocked stony bluff filled with hundreds of pits or small caves, most of them too small for a man to enter, some considerably larger where the river in bygone days had carved out passages.

"Yes," Brieux said, "that's it." Then he turned and walked away, hands behind his back.

Ziegler climbed to the wheelhouse and settled his hungry eyes on von Roenne. "In closer, the colonel says. We're going to blast them out of the caves."

"All right."

Ziegler hesitated, his dull eyes gleaming, then climbed back down, going forward eagerly to the guns. Roenne turned toward Johst and Fritzche. "Well," he asked quietly, "where do you stand?"

"With you, always with you, Captain," Johst said without hesitation.

Fritzche, sighing, slowly nodded. "As you will have it, Count von Roenne."

13

ERIC O'REILLEY EASED his position and studied the approaching boat with his field glasses. Paul Kruger lay beside him, peering from the mouth of the cave through the telescopic sight mounted on the Mannlicher .458. Behind them Gore and Henshaw crouched next to Tami, who continued to roll restlessly in his drug-induced sleep. Henshaw had been concerned only about his daughter, and Gore had seemed broken, his face scratched, his clothing ripped after a night's retreat through the thorny brush. But now both men showed new resolve as the gunboat swung toward the shore.

"Well, they know where we are, no doubt about it," O'Reilley said at last.

Kruger was placing his ammunition in neat, shiny rows at his righthand side. His face was grim, his eyes red and angry.

"What do we do?" Gore asked, crawling forward, carbine in hand.

"We'll have to—" he began, and then the four-inch guns opened up. The first shell shrieked through the air and impacted fifty feet below the cave mouth, bringing down a shower of stone and dust. Tami screamed out in his sleep and Henshaw was knocked flat on his back. The second, deafening explosion followed and Paul Kruger, shouting out curses, began firing, his rifle belching smoke, his hunter's aim taking down two SS men before they dove for cover.

O'Reilley was behind the sights of his Weatherby now, tracking onto targets, firing. He saw two more men go down, the head of one lifted from his neck by a fountain of blood.

The racket was deafening. A third and a fourth shell from the deck guns thundered into the cave-riddled bluff and the SS men stormed ashore under cover of the barrage. O'Reilley stopped one man in the water, but a dozen others, SS and regular army, had reached the shore. Kruger got another, the animal called Erzberger.

Gore and Henshaw had opened up, ineffectually for the most part, as the darting Germans moved through the brush at the base of the bluff.

O'Reilley lifted his sights to the boat, wanting to stop the pounding of the big guns. He focused on the wheelhouse, seeing von Roenne there. One bullet, and perhaps the boat would drift downriver. He had started to squeeze off that round but was transfixed by something in Roenne's manner. He could make out the pistol in the captain's hand, see him gesture to someone on the deck; and, scanning the boat, O'Reilley saw three sailors working toward the deck guns, where two SS men sat reloading.

One sailor was up and onto the gundeck, his pistol firing into the face of the nearest Schutzstaffel soldier. The second wheeled and fired his Luger five times into the sailor, but the burly engineer had clambered up the far side of the gun deck and now had his massive arms around the SS man's neck. The struggle was brief. Then, as O'Reilley watched with amazement, the chief engineer began cranking the guns down and away. Another sailor loaded as he worked, and in a few seconds the guns spoke again, sending a screaming shell into the midst of the SS men ashore. Another round followed, and another. O'Reilley could see the soldiers breaking, running, trying for the jungle beyond, and he settled in behind his sights again, snuggling up to the stock of the Weatherby, picking them off as they broke for cover.

He didn't see it happen, but Gore did, and he told him later. Olbricht, wounded through the leg, was rolling about on the ground, his lips frothing curses. There was no one to be trusted. No one but Ziegler.

"Kill him!" Olbricht screamed. "Kill that traitor!"

Another shot—one from Henshaw's gun, Gore later maintained—finished the career of Georg Olbricht, colonel, SD.

But in Ziegler's mind, his death did nothing to invalidate the order. He had been told to kill, and kill he would.

He could not use his submachine gun, but by slithering through the bush as the searching, constant gunfire continued, he was able to reach the river and slip into it. It was not an easy swim with the swift current, but Ziegler made it to the boat on the far side, clambered up, and dashed across the deck in a low crouch, his animal eyes intent.

He took a Luger from a dead soldier and cautiously crept up the ladder to the wheelhouse.

"Roenne," he said hoarsely, and when the captain turned, the Luger exploded in his face, killing him instantly only a split second before O'Reilley triggered off and saw Ziegler blown from the ladder to land on the deck and lie still, staring up at the empty African sky.

Minutes later the heavy firing from the other direction began, and in less than half an hour Mesotho had fought his way through to where O'Reilley had been trapped. The African climbed the bluff while his men searched and stripped the dead Germans; they took no prisoners.

"My son?" he asked.

"All right," Dr. Henshaw said with a dazed smile. "Tami is fine."

The German sailors, the three who remained alive, sat on the deck of the gunboat. The legionnaires, who had taken no part whatsoever in the battle, stood in a neat, white-uniformed rank along the port rail, their weapons at their feet. Brieux surrendered formally to Lord Gore.

O'Reilley spared the amoral, convictionless French commander one scathing glance and then, rifle slung across his shoulder, Paul behind him, he climbed the ladder to where von Roenne lay sprawled in a pool of his own congealing blood.

"Why?" Kruger said in amazement. "What made him do it?"

"Perhaps," O'Reilley guessed, "a sense of honor."

*   *   *

156

The war was over. Word came via a Liberian freighter whose crew was surprised that the Cameroons hadn't heard. The French had gone, and during May a Lysander aircraft landed at the repaired airfield and a British military commander arrived with several men to restore order. The Bamilekes were ordered to turn in their guns, and a few were actually recovered.

The steel box had been passed to the British consulate and was now receiving an incredulous inspection in London's Whitehall Street. But then other such documents were coming to light now, and the few survivors of the concentration camps had been interviewed, so there wasn't much novel about the report, although its depth and precision were helpful in substantiating guilt.

The paper they most coveted, the one with the signature of the Führer on it, the paper which pointed the finger of guilt toward the highest office, had somehow disappeared. No amount of searching turned it up.

They served tea in delicate china cups and whisky in fragile crystal glasses. O'Reilley stood uncomfortably in his linen suit, watching Lord Gore chat up the new British governor and his lady. Gore was returning to England to retire to "gentility and tranquillity, God allowing, for the rest of my days. I've seen Africa."

Henshaw would be staying on. His work was far from finished, probably never would be. It was a disease-ravaged land with little sanitation and much superstition. "I'll stay until Mesotho or someone like him drives me out," Dr. Henshaw said.

"What about you, Eric?" She was near him on the patio, a smile lighting her eyes, her auburn hair sun-warmed. Beyond, the sea gleamed in the late African sun. "Back to the bush for you and Paul?"

"Paul's going home. He doesn't know why, but he is going. I haven't got the will to go on hunting either. Maybe I've seen too much blood recently. Maybe," he smiled, "it's your gentle persuasion."

"Then what will you do?"

"Two choices. I can stay on and work as a guide, for one. There's always work with the anthropologists and the butterfly collectors and the bridge builders. Or," he said with a shrug, "I can give up on this bloody continent and go home. I haven't seen the States for a long while. It's up to you," he said, taking her in his arms as the red African sun began to set and the sky went to purple and crimson, "because you're going to be with me whichever it is, aren't you?"

"Yes," she barely managed to whisper. "Yes, I am."

If you have enjoyed this book and would like to receive details of other Walker Adventure titles, please write to:

Adventure Fiction Editor
Walker and Company
720 Fifth Avenue
New York, NY 10019